Praise for

A LITTLE GENTLE SLEUTHING

'A first novel by a clearly gifted and knowledgeable writer, never less than engaging and readable'
Financial Times

FINISHING TOUCH

'Gently old-fashioned whodunit, riddled with lurking anguish'
The Times

OVER THE EDGE

'She has the rare skill that grabs the reader's complete attention at page one and holds it to the end'
Wilts and Gloucestershire Standard

EXHAUSTIVE ENQUIRIES

'The gently old-fashioned style of unravelling the mystery is as riveting as any violent fast-paced novel or film'
Cotswolds Life

MALICE POETIC

'Full of sharp insights with an unexpected twist in the tail. A satisfying read'
Val McDermid, *Manchester Evening News*

DEADLY LEGACY

'As absorbing as ever . . . another intriguing and dangerous case'
Gloucestershire Echo

Also by Betty Rowlands
and available from Hodder & Stoughton paperbacks

A Little Gentle Sleuthing
Finishing Touch
Over the Edge
Exhaustive Enquiries
Malice Poetic
Deadly Legacy

About the Author

In 1988 Betty Rowlands won the Sunday Express/Veuve Clicquot Crime Short Story of the Year Competition. Her success continued with the publication of seven Melissa Craig Mysteries. She is an active member of the Crime Writers' Association and regularly gives talks and readings, runs workshops and serves on panels at Crime Writing Conventions.

She lives in the heart of the Cotswolds where her Melissa Craig mysteries are set and has three grown-up children and four grandchildren.

Smiling At Death

Betty Rowlands

NEW ENGLISH LIBRARY
Hodder and Stoughton

First published in Great Britain in 1996
by Hodder & Stoughton

First published in paperback in 1996
by Hodder & Stoughton
A division of Hodder Headline PLC

A New English Library paperback

10 9 8 7 6 5 4 3 2 1

British Library CIP

Rowlands, Betty
Smiling at death. – (A Melissa Craig mystery)
1. English fiction – 20th century
I. Title II. Series
823.9′14[F]

ISBN 0 340 66048 1

Printed and bound in Great Britain by
Cox & Wyman Ltd, Reading, Berkshire

Hodder and Stoughton
A division of Hodder Headline PLC
338 Euston Road
London NW1 3BH

To Maggie Body,
who taught me so much about the
craft of crime writing.

Prologue

The following report appeared in the *Gloucester Gazette* on 8 January:

VILLAGE OF FEAR

Residents Hide Behind Wall of Silence

Following the third murder within six months of a local resident in her own home, the population of the village of Thanebury is living in fear. All the victims were found suffocated in their beds, all were frail, elderly and living alone. In no case was there any sign of forced entry, and nothing was stolen. At a recent news conference, Detective Superintendent Ivor Thoroughgood, who is leading the investigation, stated, 'There appears to be a very sick mind at work here, whose motive is at present a mystery to us. We appeal to any member of the public who may have seen anyone acting suspiciously near the homes of these unfortunate people to come forward. Meanwhile, we would urge everyone to take extra care to secure their property and not to admit any unauthorised person into their homes.'

It is understood that so far there has been no response to the police appeal for information. Local residents, when approached by the press, take refuge behind a wall of silence. There is fear in their eyes and one senses that something is being concealed, but no one will speak of it.

Chapter One

One Friday morning in early March, Kenneth Harris, recently retired after thirty years' service in the Gloucestershire Constabulary and now sole proprietor of Harris Investigations, glanced up from the report he was writing as Tricia Jessop, his young assistant, entered his office and closed the door behind her.

'Mrs Aggs is here,' she announced.

Harris frowned and glanced at his watch. 'She's not due till eleven and it's only ten to,' he muttered irritably. 'I was hoping to finish this first.'

'I warned her she might have to wait a while, but she's been here five minutes already and she's beginning to fidget. I'm afraid she'll chicken out if you don't see her soon.'

'Any idea what it's about?'

'Oh yes, it's matrimonial.' Tricia's voice lowered discreetly as she added, 'She thinks hubby's been "up to something".'

'Such as what?'

'Having it off with another woman, I suppose.' Tricia glanced over her shoulder to satisfy herself that the door was properly closed. 'Can't say I'd blame him – she's a . . .'

'She's a client, and we don't make personal remarks

about clients,' Harris interrupted. 'Has she told you why she suspects him?'

Tricia had been in the job for only a few months, but she had already demonstrated that she was more than just a pretty face under a mop of curly auburn hair. She had a friendly manner and a sympathetic personality that put nervous clients at their ease. Some of them seemed to think consulting a private detective was vaguely disreputable, and occasionally showed signs of a last minute change of heart. Tricia's soothing approach inspired confidence and had, Harris suspected, been instrumental in retaining several lucrative commissions which might otherwise have been lost. It was, he had observed, chiefly women with straying husbands who tended to pour out their troubles to her, telling her things they were too shy to confess directly to him. Men were more likely to make a pass at her . . . and she knew how to handle that, too.

It emerged that Mrs Aggs had revealed only so much.

'She says she found "something" in his pocket.' Tricia gave a knowing look.

'Condoms?'

'I imagine so, but she wouldn't be specific. Says it's too embarrassing.'

'If she won't tell you, she's hardly likely to tell me.' Harris sighed and slid the report into a drawer. 'Okay, ask her to come in.'

'Right.'

He stood up to greet Mrs Aggs and waited while she lowered herself gingerly onto the edge of the chair facing his. He judged her to be in her fifties, a plain, gaunt woman with a humourless expression. Her face had a scrubbed appearance and she was unbecomingly dressed in a tweed suit of an indeterminate shade of brown. On her head was a round velour hat with a turned-up brim, similar in style to one that Tricia sometimes wore. On the younger woman, it looked charming; on Mrs Aggs, it resembled an inverted chamber-pot. Harris had a mischievous desire, hastily stifled, to get up and walk behind her to see if it had a handle. It was, he thought as he sat down again, hardly surprising that her husband should seek his pleasure elsewhere . . . he put a hand to his mouth and cleared his throat.

'Well, Mrs Aggs, how can I help you?' he said.

'It's Mr Aggs,' she replied. 'He's been with another woman.' The words tumbled out in a rush, as if she had learned them by heart and feared she might forget them.

'What makes you think that?'

'He sneaks off during the night when he thinks I'm asleep.'

'Where does he go?'

Mrs Aggs gave him a withering stare. 'That's what I expect you to find out. All he tells me is, he can't sleep and goes out for a drive.'

'Does he say why he can't sleep? Has he any financial worries, for example?'

'Certainly not!' Mrs Aggs seemed to find the very idea offensive.

'How long is he absent on these occasions?'

'Not long. An hour, maybe.'

'How often does this happen?'

'I've woken up twice to find him missing. The first time, I believed his story. The second time, I wasn't so sure. And now I'm wondering if there were other times when I didn't wake up, when I didn't know he'd been out.'

'When was the last time this happened?'

'It was the night of the sixth of December.'

'And before that?'

'About two months earlier.'

Harris sat back and spread his large hands, palms upwards, on the desk. 'That hardly points to a grand passion, does it, Mrs Aggs?' He adopted the soothing tone which he had used in the past when dealing with a nervous witness to a crime. 'Are you absolutely certain he isn't telling the truth?'

'Why should he suddenly start suffering from insomnia, after sleeping like a baby every night of his life?'

'He may have problems at work that he doesn't like to bother you with.'

'He's always been very open with me about everything until now.'

Harris waited for a few moments. From what Tricia had told him, he knew that there was more to come. It was evident that Mrs Aggs was finding the interview painful. Years of questioning suspects had taught him to spot the tell-tale signs that something was being concealed: the restless hands, the uncontrollable twitch of facial muscles, the reluctance to look him straight in the eye. Mrs Aggs was showing all these. He tried again.

'These bouts of sleeplessness – let's call them that for the moment,' he added as Mrs Aggs opened her colourless mouth to protest, 'are they the only reason you have . . .'

'That's just it,' she interrupted. 'I found,' she hesitated, swallowed, and looked away again, 'something in his pocket. Something that could only belong to a woman.'

So it wasn't condoms. A handkerchief, perhaps . . . or frilly knickers. For a split second he found himself speculating on the kind of underwear Mrs Aggs favoured; then, telling himself not to be frivolous, he asked, 'Did you ask your husband how this, er, article came to be in his pocket?'

'I did. He concocted some ridiculous story of having found it on the office floor after all the girls had gone home. He said if he'd left it on a desk, one of the cleaners might have stolen it.'

'And this is all the evidence you have that your husband is being unfaithful to you?'

Mrs Aggs dropped her eyes and began fiddling with the clasp of her brown leather handbag. 'Yes,' she whispered. 'That's why I've come to you.'

Harris glanced at the clock. Already this unattractive, neurotic creature had wasted nearly half an hour of his time; he had an urgent report to write, telephone calls to make and another appointment before lunch. Then he told himself he was being unkind; her problem might seem trivial, even faintly comic to him, but to her it was deadly serious.

'Are you sure a private investigator is the best person to handle your problems?' he said. 'It seems to me this is more a case for a marriage guidance expert, or . . . are you and your husband active church members? Perhaps you could have a word with your vicar?'

The suggestion appeared to throw Mrs Aggs into a state of agitation, barely controlled. 'I couldn't possibly tell the Reverend Jarman,' she faltered.

'Then why not try a professional counsellor? My assistant can give you an address.'

'I don't want counselling. I want him followed.' In contrast to her previous hesitant manner, her voice took on an unexpected ring of determination.

Harris drew a deep breath in an effort to contain his rising exasperation. 'Mrs Aggs, you have told me nothing to convince me that your husband is having an affair. Now, if there had been suspicious telephone calls, or if he'd been coming home late with lipstick on his collar, or if it had been contraceptives you found in his pocket . . .'

Mrs Aggs got to her feet. 'Thank you, that's quite enough,' she said. 'It's obvious I can expect no help from you.'

'I apologise if I've upset you.' He stood up and moved round the desk as she made for the door. 'When we're dealing with, er, matrimonial misdemeanours,' – he knew instinctively that the word 'adultery' would also give offence – 'we have to face unpleasant possibilities.'

Mrs Aggs hesitated. Despite her unprepossessing appearance, he felt a certain sympathy for her. She was obviously a deeply unhappy woman.

'These nocturnal outings your husband makes,' he went on, 'do they happen at particular times? Can you connect them with anything else?'

She had her back towards him, but he saw her stiffen at the final question.

'What do you mean?' she asked, without turning round.

'I was thinking of something like a phone call a few hours beforehand, or a letter that seemed to disturb him.'

'Oh no, nothing like that,' she said, but her voice was uncertain and the tension was still there. Then, with what seemed a great effort, she swung round to face him again.

'I want him followed,' she repeated. 'Next time he goes

out, I want you to find out where he goes . . . and what he does.'

'How will I know when that's likely to be?'

Mrs Aggs stared down at her feet. 'Thinking back, I remember him being quiet and withdrawn around the last time it happened. Perhaps if I notice anything like that again, I could let you know . . . then you could keep watch near our house and go after him . . . could you do that?'

'I could, if that's what you want, but if I had to wait for several nights before anything happened it would be very expensive.'

'How much?'

Harris was fast losing interest in Mrs Aggs and her problems. He didn't really want this job. He named a figure which he was confident would frighten her off. She looked startled, but did not, as he had hoped, backtrack immediately.

'I'll think about it and let you know,' she said, and left.

With a shrug, Harris returned to his desk and got out his report, but he had barely opened the file before there was a light knock and Melissa Craig entered. His irritation evaporated at the sight of her.

'Darling, you look great. Love the hairdo,' he said.

Melissa patted the glossy brown knot on the crown of her head with a smile of satisfaction.

'Thanks, I've just had it done.' She sank into the chair that Mrs Aggs had recently vacated, breathing a little heavily. 'I wish this office wasn't at the top of four flights of stairs,' she complained.

'All I can afford at present. Cheltenham's not cheap.'

'No, I suppose not.'

'I get a nice view of the gardens,' he pointed out. 'Not that I get much time to look out of the window,' he added, seeing her raised eyebrow.

'I'm glad to hear it. Have you had a busy week?'

'Not bad at all. Considering I've been in business less than twelve months, I can't complain.'

'Was that angry-looking lady I met on the stairs a client?'

'I hope not. I've a feeling she'd be more trouble than she's worth.'

'What's her problem – an erring husband?'

'So she claims. My guess is, it's all in her mind.'

'Poor woman,' said Melissa. 'She's not exactly a raver, is she? Although you never know, she might be very sexy under that formidable exterior.'

'I prefer your exterior . . . and your brand of sexiness.' His hand reached across the desk for hers and he leaned forward to kiss her, but she hastily disengaged.

'Not in the office,' she said firmly.

'As you say. What have you been doing in town?'

'Shopping, hairdresser, posting off proofs.'

'Another successful case for Nathan Latimer?'

'I'm afraid so.'

'Why "afraid"?'

Melissa got up and began prowling round the office. 'Sometimes I think it's time for a change of direction,' she said. 'I've written twenty crime novels and I'm not sure I can go on indefinitely.' She gave a sudden, mischievous smile. 'Perhaps I could try my hand at the real thing. How would you like to take me on as a partner? Harris and Craig, Crime Busters Inc?'

He chuckled. 'You'd hate it. It can get pretty tedious, trailing some nerd who claims to have an injured leg in the hope that he'll give himself away by jumping on a moving bus . . . or snapping erring husbands sneaking in and out of seedy hotels with their secretaries.'

'You make it sound a real drag. Are you beginning to have regrets?'

'No, of course not. Mind you, the odd bit of skulduggery would liven things up a bit.' His glance swerved briefly towards the door as he confided, 'Tricia's longing for what she calls "a really juicy case"!'

Melissa laughed and got to her feet. 'I'll be on my way. You won't forget the Fords' drinks party on Sunday, will you?'

He pulled a face. 'Do I have to go? These lunchtime chatter sessions aren't really my scene.'

'I know, but Iris is still in France and it'll be such a drag on my own. Please, Ken.'

'Okay, I'll be there, but I'll need a stiffener before I face the mob.'

'Call for me in good time and you shall have one.'

Chapter Two

Across the crowded, low-ceilinged sitting-room of Tanners Cottage, Melissa caught Ken Harris's eye and read in it a plea for rescue. Major Dudley Ford, his normally florid cheeks flushed almost purple from the combined effects of heat and wine, was holding forth with great energy and many forceful gestures of the bottles he was holding. The noise level created by upwards of thirty people trying to carry on a dozen different conversations in a confined space made it impossible for Melissa to make out what their irascible host was saying, but she would have laid a sizeable bet that he was repeating his well-known views on the treatment of criminals. A good taste of old-fashioned military discipline for petty thieves, flogging for muggers, hanging for killers – she, and almost everyone else in the village, had heard it many times. Poor old Ken, she thought. Being temporarily disengaged, she began to edge her way through the throng, only to be waylaid by the major's wife, Madeleine, who thrust a silver tray of canapés under her nose.

'We're *so* glad Mr Harris is able to be with us today,' she purred, with a glance in the direction of her husband and his captive. 'It must make life so much *easier* for you, now that he's retired from the police.'

'Easier? In what way?'

For a moment, Mrs Ford appeared nonplussed at the directness of the question. The enamelled smile on her carefully made-up features wavered, then burst out again with a renewed radiance that held a hint of archness.

'I remember so well what a difference it made when Dudley retired from the army,' she explained. 'The uncertainty was gone . . . that feeling of never being sure where he'd be this time next month, or how long he'd be away . . . that sort of thing makes a relationship quite . . . tricky at times. Didn't you find that . . . with your, er, friend,' – the word was accompanied by another meaning smile – 'with the irregular hours and so on?'

'I can't say I did,' said Melissa in her most matter-of-fact tone. 'Ken and I don't live together, you know, so the problem didn't arise.'

'Oh, of *course* not. I'm sure I didn't mean to imply anything *improper* . . .'

Oh yes you did, you nosey old witch, thought Melissa, helping herself to a vol-au-vent, *and you shouldn't wear that shade of green, it makes you look bilious*. Aloud, she said, 'Madeleine, these are absolutely delicious – please take them away or I'll scoff the lot!'

'You're right, they're *superb*!' A tall, slim young woman with strong features and large dark eyes, emerging from the crush to join them, reached for a smoked salmon roulade with mulberry-tipped fingers that matched her clinging woollen dress. 'It was so kind of you and your husband to invite us when we've only lived here such a short time,' she said, before popping the morsel into her mouth.

'My dear, Miss Donovan, we're delighted to have the opportunity to get to know you a little better . . . and so glad you were able to persuade your father . . . do you know Mrs Craig?' Madeleine's rather prominent eyes swivelled to and fro. 'In fact,' she added effusively, 'she's Mel Craig, the crime writer, our local celebrity. We're very proud of her.'

'Take no notice of the label,' said the 'celebrity' with a smile. 'In Upper Benbury, I'm just another resident. And please, don't let's be formal – my name's Melissa.'

'And I'm Sirry. My father called me Cerulean and my younger sister's Magenta, but we're known as Sirry and Genty,' explained the elder Miss Donovan.

'Such *unusual* names, don't you think?' cooed Madeleine. By intonation, she implied that 'unusual' was synonymous with 'bizarre', but Sirry merely nodded, swallowed her roulade and helped herself to another.

'Such an *original* notion,' Madeleine gushed. 'Artists have such . . . *inspiration*, don't you agree, Melissa?' She turned back to Sirry. 'There are just the two of you?'

'We had a brother, Saxe.'

'Ah yes, Saxe blue. How quaint!' Madeleine gave a high-pitched laugh that reminded Melissa of breaking glass. She seemed not to have noticed the past tense, nor the shadow that passed across Sirry's face. 'Quite a spectrum, in fact,' she continued brightly. 'Well, I'll leave you two to chat.' With her tray elegantly poised on an upturned palm, she disappeared into the crowd.

'How are you settling in?' asked Melissa, after a pause during which Sirry's thoughts seemed far away.

'All right, I suppose.' She stared at the drink she was holding. 'Genty and I have been looking out for Iris Ash,' she said after another pause, 'I believe she's a friend of yours?'

'That's right. She owns the cottage next to mine, but she's away at the moment.'

'We hoped she'd be here. We think it would do Father good to have a fellow artist to talk to.'

'She's in Provence, she goes there every winter,' Melissa explained. 'She'll be back in a couple of weeks or so. I wrote and told her you'd moved into the village and she's particularly looking forward to meeting your father. She says he was one of her tutors at art college.'

'Really?' Sirry's face lit up. 'I daresay he'll remember her. He has a phenomenal memory for people he's met . . . or rather, he used to have.' Her voice dropped and her smile faded as, for the second time, some unspoken thought dulled the brightness of her eyes.

'So your father is here?' Melissa was curious to meet the man who, because of his reclusive habits, had become the focus of a certain amount of local curiosity.

'He's over by the window. Genty's with him.' Sirry gestured with her wineglass to where a handsome, sandy-haired man of about seventy was staring vacantly into the crowd, taking no apparent notice of the dark-haired young woman at his side. A brooding expression came over Sirry's face and for several seconds she was silent, her gaze fixed on her father and sister.

In an attempt to get the conversation going again, Melissa commented, 'You and Genty are very much alike. I suppose you take after your mother?'

Sirry nodded absently. 'We get our looks from her, yes.'

'She's not here today?'

'She's staying with her family in Warsaw. She . . . finds it difficult since Saxe died . . . he was like Father in looks, but he had Mama's temperament . . . they were very close.' Sirry blinked in an effort to disperse unshed tears.

'His death must have been a terrible blow for all of you,' said Melissa gently. After a pause, she said, 'I understand from Iris that your father's work is very well known.'

Sirry sighed and stared down into the empty wineglass. 'He hasn't picked up a brush or a pencil since Saxe died. We were hoping that the move to Gloucestershire . . . Hampstead was so full of memories . . . we thought perhaps a change of scene . . . but it's as if the light has gone out of his life.' She raised her eyes on the final words. The pain was back, and with it a hint of some other emotion that Melissa could not identify.

At this point, they were approached by the rector's wife, Alice Hamley, who asked, 'Has either of you seen Miss Willis? I wanted to have a word about the church flowers.'

Melissa shook her head. 'Martha? No, I haven't. Perhaps she's gone home.'

'I'm not sure she's been here. No one else seems to have seen her.'

'That's odd,' said Sirry. 'She said she was coming when I spoke to her yesterday. She was looking forward to it. We offered her a lift, but she said if it was fine she'd rather walk. I wonder where she's got to?'

'Perhaps she felt too tired. Never mind, I'll give her a ring presently,' said Alice. 'And how are you all settling in at Larkfield Barn?' she asked chattily.

Sirry made a polite reply, which elicited a further question. Melissa took the opportunity to slip away and rejoin Ken Harris, who by this time had escaped from Dudley Ford and, by coincidence, moved across to the window where she found him in conversation with Sirry's father and sister.

'You must be Mr Donovan,' she said. 'I'm Melissa

Craig, I've just been talking to your other daughter.' She held out a hand and he took it a little hesitantly. His smile seemed to cost considerable effort.

'Call me Cluny.' he said. 'I know what you're thinking,' he went on, and over a certain lifeless quality in his tone, she caught a hint of an Irish accent. ''Tis a strange name for a man, but me mother insisted on it. 'Twas there at the abbey that she felt me stirring in her womb for the first time. She wouldn't hear of me being called anything else.' He had evidently told the story many times, for he spoke the words mechanically, like a child repeating a lesson.

His younger daughter held out her hand to Melissa. She had the same brilliant, flashing smile as her sister. 'I'm Genty,' she said. 'Now that you've heard the family legend, consider us acquainted.'

'Where's Sirry?' There was a hint of alarm in Cluny's voice as his eyes searched the room. 'I don't see her, Genty . . . where's Sirry?'

'I left her talking to the rector's wife,' said Melissa.

'She shouldn't go wandering off like that . . .'

'Hush, Father, she'll be here in a minute . . . yes, here she is.'

'I see you've met Melissa,' said Sirry as she rejoined them. 'We've had such an interesting chat. Did you know, Melissa's a famous crime writer, Father?'

'A writer, eh?' For the first time, Cluny showed a glimmer of interest. 'An excellent craft, to be sure. Needs a lot of practice, of course. Plenty of practice,' he reiterated as Melissa smiled and nodded. 'Practice makes perfect. Isn't that right, me darlings? Haven't I always said that? Practice makes perfect.'

'That's quite right, Father. Practice makes perfect,' chanted the sisters in unison. They looked first at their father and then at one another, exchanging mysterious half-smiles like children with a secret. Then, as if remembering that they were not alone, Genty tugged at Cluny's arm and said, 'We really should be leaving. Our table's booked for half-past one.'

'They're taking me to some fancy restaurant,' Cluny explained and passively allowed himself to be led away.

'What a rum family,' commented Ken Harris, who had remained silent throughout the exchanges. He took Melissa's hand. 'Can we leave as well? What's for lunch? I'm starving.'

'Starving? After all those canapés I saw you wolfing?'

'Not enough to keep a bird alive. Come on, before that old war-horse starts bending my ear again.'

'We can't sneak off without saying goodbye.'

'Then let's get on with it. There's Mrs War-horse, over by the door.' He made his way purposefully through the crush with Melissa in his wake. 'Thank you so much, it was a lovely party,' he said.

Madeleine treated him to one of her most gracious smiles. 'I'm *so* glad you were able to come,' she purred. 'Melissa, I wonder if you'd mind calling on Miss Willis as you go home, just to make sure she's all right. I'm a little concerned about her.'

'Of course we don't mind, do we, Ken?'

'Glad of the exercise.' He patted his stomach. 'Help to walk down all those delicious goodies!'

'You old humbug!' Melissa hissed as they made their way to the front door.

'Not going already?' Major Ford emerged from the kitchen with two newly-opened bottles. 'Pity. Have to carry on our discussion another time, eh?'

'I look forward to it,' responded Harris politely.

'What was that about?' asked Melissa as they set off. 'No, don't tell me. The breakdown of law and order . . . all down to wishy-washy, left-wing do-gooders . . .'

He chuckled. 'Something like that. Plus a bit of local gossip. The old boy's very intrigued with the Donovans – especially the daughters. He called them "a pair of smart little fillies".'

'The old sexist!'

'The father seems a bit odd – in fact, they all do.'

'There was a brother who died. It seems to have had a shattering effect on the whole family.'

'What do the girls do?'

'I heard that one of them – I'm not sure which – teaches part time at the art college in Cheltenham. The other one stays home and looks after the old man. They've only lived here a couple of months or so.'

They had reached the end of the track leading to Melissa's cottage and Harris automatically changed direction, but Melissa grasped his arm. 'We're going to check on Miss Willis, remember?'

'Do we have to? You're not seriously worried about the old duck, are you?'

'That's not the point: I promised. Besides, she could have been taken ill – she had a heart attack some while ago and she still suffers from angina.'

'Oh, very well.'

'It isn't far.'

It was a mere quarter of a mile, but it was uphill and by the time they reached Martha Willis's cottage, Harris was puffing. 'You're out of condition,' said Melissa severely. 'Not enough exercise. Here we are.'

'Pretty little place,' he commented. 'A bit isolated, though.'

'Especially for an old person living alone,' agreed Melissa. 'Martha's been a lot happier since the Donovans arrived. Larkfield Barn is just up the lane.' She pointed to a stone building, half hidden behind a clump of trees.

Harris gave a disinterested nod and put his hands in his pockets. 'I'll wait here for you.'

'As you like.' Melissa pushed open the gate and walked up the short path to the front door. There was no bell, so she rapped with her knuckles. No response. She rattled the letter-box, then bent down and shouted through the slot. Still no answer.

'Try the back door,' advised Harris, leaning on the gate.

The back door was closed, but unlocked. It led straight into the kitchen. With her hand on the latch, Melissa called again, 'Miss Willis, are you there? It's Melissa Craig.' Silence. She stepped inside, called again, and listened. There was no sound in the house but the whirr of the central heating pump and the tick of the old-fashioned clock on the wooden dresser.

With increasing urgency, she repeated her call. She opened the door leading into the hallway, half expecting, half fearing to see a motionless form on the floor, but there was nothing. She checked the two downstairs rooms and then, after a moment's hesitation, climbed the narrow staircase.

There were three doors leading off the tiny landing and they were all closed so that the only light came from a reeded glass panel in the front door. Melissa called yet again, then knocked gently on one door. No one answered, so she opened it and looked inside. A bathroom, empty. She tried the next one, which faced the stairs. A cupboard, its shelves piled with neatly folded linen.

The third door was slightly ajar. Melissa knocked, then gingerly pushed it further open. The curtains were closed, but in the light filtering round the edges she could make out the furniture: a wardrobe, a dressing table, a bed . . . not empty.

Her heart thumping with apprehension, she ran to the window, dragged the curtains apart and swung round. For several seconds she stood staring in mute horror at the thing in the bed. Then she screamed.

Chapter Three

By the time Ken reached her, Melissa was in the bathroom with her head over the handbasin, retching violently. He held her head until the spasms subsided, then filled a tumbler with water and put it into her shaking hand. She rinsed out her mouth and then allowed herself to be steered to a chair where she sat shivering uncontrollably.

'Oh Ken, it's revolting . . . sick . . .'

'What is?'

Melissa pointed through the open door to the room across the landing from which she had just fled, nauseated with shock. 'In there . . . she's dead . . . and her face has been painted . . . like a clown's!'

'Oh, no!' he muttered. 'Not another.'

'What do you mean?' she asked through chattering teeth, but he ignored the question and said, 'You're cold. Have this.' He took off his coat and put it round her shoulders. She pulled it close, comforted by the residual warmth from his body. 'I'm going to leave you for a moment,' he told her. 'Stay there till I come back.'

The command was unnecessary. The last thing she wanted was to return to the room where lay the most gruesome sight she had ever seen. She sat huddled under the weight of the heavy woollen coat, taking deep breaths in an effort to steady herself. After a few moments her internal organs settled to something like their normal rhythm, but nothing could blot out the hideous memory of the dead woman's face, the eyes wide and staring, the ghastly rictus painted in red on flesh turned blue. Blue . . . that meant suffocation, didn't it? And what had Ken meant when he exclaimed, 'Not another?' Had a serial killer struck in her quiet Cotswold village? The thought filled her with dread.

He was soon back. Without a word, he dived into the pocket of the coat that she was still clutching round her shoulders and took out his cellphone. He tapped out a number, spoke briefly to whoever answered, and waited, hugging her close with his free arm. Thankfully, she leaned against him. 'Okay now?' he said.

'Yes, I'm fine.'

'Did you touch anything?'

'Only door handles.'

'Good.' He began a brief exchange with someone at the end of the line. She heard him giving directions for reaching the cottage, then he snapped down the aerial and put the phone away.

'The lads will be here soon. We'll wait downstairs, if you like.'

'Please.'

They went back to the kitchen. On either side of a small table were two old-fashioned wooden chairs with cushions covered to match the blue-checked gingham tablecloth. They sat for a few moments without speaking; it seemed to Melissa as if the entire village must have been reduced to a stunned silence by the foul deed committed on its doorstep. Then, like sound effects gradually faded in, she became aware of background noises: the sonorous tick of the clock, the throb of a tractor in a neighbouring field, the chatter of starlings on the roof and the subdued hum of Martha's central heating system.

Suddenly, Harris got up to inspect the boiler.

'What are you doing?' she asked.

'Just checking.' He peered at the controls. 'The system's set to come on automatically at six o'clock.' He glanced at his watch. 'That means it's been running for approximately eight hours.'

'What does that tell you?'

'Me, not a lot, but it may help the medics to establish the time of death. The bedroom was quite warm, did you notice?'

'I can't say I did. There was something else to grab my attention.' Melissa shuddered as the memory returned afresh. 'Ken, when you said "Not another" just now, what did you mean?'

He returned to his chair. His expression was grim. 'There's been a maniac on the loose during the past few months in the Thanebury area, preying on elderly people living alone. He enters their houses at night without doing any damage or disturbing or stealing anything, just quietly suffocates his victims in their beds. You must have seen the reports.'

'Yes, of course, but the victims didn't have clown's faces painted on them, did they?'

He hesitated for a moment before saying, 'They each had a huge smile painted in lipstick round the mouth – just like that poor old lady in there.'

Melissa felt her gorge rising again. She put a hand to her mouth and took a couple of deep breaths to steady herself. 'Whoever does that must be very sick indeed,' she whispered. 'Have the police any idea . . . ?'

'Not so far as I know.'

'There hasn't been anything in the papers about the . . . the smile.' It was all she could do to speak the word.

'That particular piece of information has been withheld from the press, for two reasons. One, to avoid sensationalist reports that would scare the life out of every elderly person living alone within miles. The other, to discourage potential copycats. There are some pretty weird people around these days.'

'How come you know all this? You've been out of the Force for months.'

A faint grin crumpled the ex-policeman's lumpy features. 'I still keep in touch with a few old buddies.' He glanced at his watch again and stood up. 'The boys should be here any minute. I'll go and look out for them. Why don't you put the kettle on and make a hot drink? You look as if you could use one.'

'Is that all right? I mean, I thought we weren't supposed to touch anything.'

'There's nothing in here for the SOCOS to find. Besides, she left everything ready for her early morning cuppa.' He pointed to the dresser, where a tray was set out with a teapot, one cup and saucer and an empty milk jug, all neatly arranged on an embroidered tray-cloth. On a shelf were three pottery jars labelled 'Tea', 'Sugar' and 'Coffee'. The poignant reminder of how Martha Willis's quiet, orderly life had been so brutally cut short brought a spurt of tears to Melissa's eyes. Mechanically, she filled the kettle, set it on the stove, lit the gas and waited.

It had just come to the boil when she heard the sound of a car outside, followed by men's voices. Seconds later, Harris returned with two men, one a middle-aged, uniformed officer, the other younger, sandy-haired, wearing a shapeless woollen sweater and corduroy trousers.

'Melissa, this is . . . ,' Harris began, but the younger man pushed past him, saying brusquely, 'Good morning, Madam. Acting Chief Inspector Holloway and Sergeant Mellor.' Over his shoulder he said curtly, 'Upstairs, you said, Harris? That's through here, I take it.' He pointed to the door leading to the passage. 'I assume nothing's been touched?'

Melissa saw Ken's jaw tighten as he replied, 'In the room where we found the body, nothing except for the curtains being opened. Mrs Craig was feeling unwell, so there's been a slight disturbance in the bathroom. I'll show you . . .' He took a step forward, but was waved back.

'No need for you to come up. I'll talk to you both in a minute or two.' Holloway pushed open the door and marched through, his sergeant at his heels. There came the thump of footsteps on the staircase and across the landing, followed by muffled voices.

'The kettle's boiled,' said Melissa. 'Shall I make tea or coffee?'

'Coffee. Black and strong.'

Melissa took the jar from the dresser. Harris sat down, scowling.

'Arrogant young bastard,' he muttered. 'I taught him all he knows. This time last year he was calling me Sir and now he's chucking his weight about as if he was a Super.'

'I seem to recall once saying something to you on those lines, and you assured me he was a very experienced officer,' said Melissa.

'Huh? Of course, you've had dealings with him before. Well, I stand by that – he *is* very experienced. He's a good detective all right. Not in the best of tempers at the moment, though.'

Melissa put two cups of black coffee on the table and sat down. 'Why's that?'

'Officially, he's not on duty, but they called him out because everyone else is either off sick or otherwise engaged.'

They were halfway through their coffee when the two policemen returned. 'What's this?' Holloway demanded. 'I don't remember giving permission . . .'

'Mrs Craig was badly shaken by her experience so I suggested . . .' Harris began, but was interrupted for the second time.

'Nothing should have been touched until the SOCOS have finished,' said Holloway officiously.

'Oh, for God's sake, Des, come off your high horse! It's perfectly obvious the killer went straight through here and upstairs. There wasn't a teaspoon out of place.'

For a moment, Melissa was afraid there was going to be a slanging match. Holloway's face turned a dull red and his rather wooden features set in a resentful glare, but all he said was, 'If I could just take a few essential details, I'll get you both to come to the station tomorrow to make your formal statements. You arrived here at what time?'

The brief interview ended just as more police vehicles were arriving. With an unsmiling, 'Thank you, that will be all for now,' Holloway went out to meet them. Sergeant Mellor closed his notebook and put it in his pocket.

'How are things?' Harris asked him.

'Pretty much as usual, thank you Sir,' Mellor replied, with a wry grin. 'How about you?'

'Not bad. Could have done without this. By the way, you don't have to call me Sir any more.'

Mellor grinned again. 'No, Sir,' he said, and hurried after his superior officer as Harris turned to Melissa.

'Ready?'

'Shouldn't we wash the cups and saucers?'

'Certainly not. His lordship might want them dusted for prints.' He gave a malicious, gravelly chuckle. 'Let's go.'

After a belated lunch, for which Melissa had little appetite but which Ken tucked into with his usual relish, they went for a stroll along the valley footpath that ran past her home and linked the neighbouring villages of Upper and Lower Benbury. It was well past four o'clock; the sun was low in a clear sky and the still air held a foretaste of an overnight frost.

They had not spoken of the tragedy since leaving Martha's cottage; in fact, they had said very little. Harris had appeared abstracted and Melissa knew that, despite being no longer in the Force, he could not break the habit of thirty years. She had not been present when he went to Martha's room, but she knew that his eyes would have recorded every detail. Now, no doubt, he was mentally sifting through everything he had seen.

She slipped her arm through his. 'Penny for them.'

'Just turning a few things over in my mind.'

'What things.'

'Nothing specific.' He gave her arm a squeeze.

'I think I can guess. You're plotting ways of getting back at young Hollowhead.'

'Certainly not . . . at least . . .'

'At least what?'

'As I said, nothing specific. Shall we turn back? The sun's nearly gone down.'

'Right.' There was no point in questioning him further;

if there was anything to tell, it would be told in his own good time.

In the gathering dusk, they made their way back to Hawthorn Cottage. They had been indoors for only a few minutes when the telephone rang. An anxious Sirry Donovan was on the line.

'Melissa, what's going on? We've only just got back and there's a police car outside Martha's cottage. Has there been an accident?'

'No accident, Sirry. Martha's dead. She's been murdered. Ken and I found her.'

'Murdered . . . how?' Sirry's voice was a faint, shocked whisper.

Harris put a hand on Melissa's arm and a finger to his lips. She grasped his meaning instantly.

'There'll have to be a post mortem to establish the cause of death,' she said into the phone.

'I can't believe it,' said Sirry with a catch in her voice. 'Whoever would want to kill Martha? Do the police suspect anyone . . . did the murderer leave any clues?'

'Look, Sirry,' Melissa said as Harris made gestures to her to end the conversation. 'I'd rather not talk about it any more at the moment, if you don't mind. I'm feeling pretty upset . . . and in any case, I don't think I should discuss it until I've made my formal statement.'

'Oh, please forgive me . . . of course, it must have been an awful shock for you,' Sirry apologised. 'What a mercy your friend was with you.'

'Yes, wasn't it. Look, Sirry, I don't want to be rude, but . . .'

'I won't keep you . . . it's just . . . we were so fond of Martha . . . Melissa, if you should happen to speak to Father, please don't say anything about murder. We'll just say she died in her sleep – she did have a dodgy heart after all – then he won't get upset. He never reads the papers . . . you do understand, don't you? After what happened to our brother . . .'

'Yes, of course, I won't say a word. Goodbye.'

'Goodbye.'

Melissa exhaled slowly as she put the phone down. 'Oh dear, I'm afraid there's going to be a lot of this, once it gets around that I found Martha.'

'Don't think about that now. What about some tea?'

They went into the kitchen. Ken filled the kettle while Melissa closed the curtains. It was practically dark. It was during the hours of darkness that the killer did his deadly work. His victims were all people living alone. She herself was such a person. Younger than the others, it was true, but . . . reason began to give way to panic . . . who could tell what perverted impulse directed his choice? He had never before struck two nights running . . . but there was always a first time. Maybe he was getting a taste for it . . . a taste for death . . . that was the title of a P. D. James novel, wasn't it . . . what a laugh . . . for God's sake, Melissa, you're getting hysterical . . . suddenly she was sobbing uncontrollably.

'Mel, it's all right, you're all right.' Ken held her close while he stroked her hair, murmuring soothing words and endearments that would normally have struck her as incongruous when spoken in his gruff, gravelly voice, but which now brought comfort beyond description.

When she was calmer, he led her to a chair. She took his hand – large and sprawling and powerful, just like the rest of him, she thought in a surge of tenderness – and held it to her cheek.

'Better now?' She nodded and managed a feeble smile.

He poured two mugs of strong tea and put them on the table. She clasped one in both hands, grateful for its warmth.

Presently, they watched the early evening news on the television, but there was no mention of the murder.

'Wait till tomorrow, after the press briefing,' Harris commented. 'They'll be here like a pack of hungry wolves.'

After the news they listened to music and read the Sunday papers. Then he said he was hungry again and they went back to the kitchen while she prepared sandwiches and coffee. At ten o'clock, he said, 'I've got a busy day tomorrow, I should be going . . . unless . . .'

Panic returned and thumped her in the stomach. Without thinking, she said urgently, 'No, don't go, don't leave me alone.'

Many times before, after they had made love, he had asked to stay the night, but she had always refused. It had seemed to represent an irrevocable step, a further inroad into the independence that meant so much to her, a commitment that she was not yet ready to make. Just the same, she had known for a long time that, sooner or later, it was bound to happen. Tonight, she needed him. If it meant that she was burning her boats, so be it.

She reached out to him. 'I want you to stay,' she said.

Chapter Four

There was a sharp overnight frost. On leaving home the following morning, Melissa stood for a few moments outside her front door and contemplated the familiar, well-loved scene. No matter what the season, in fair weather or foul, alone or in company, she seldom failed to experience a sense of thankfulness for the happy chance that had brought her to this place at this particular period of her life.

Habitually peaceful, this morning it seemed unnaturally so, as if something more sinister than a coating of rime had settled on the familiar landscape of fields and woodland and dry-stone walls. Nothing stirred. There was no noise of traffic in the lane, no movement of bird or beast, no aircraft overhead. It was as if shock waves from Martha's death had reached out to all living things, warning them to be still as a mark of respect. Melissa felt a prickle of gooseflesh, then mentally chided herself for entertaining such a superstitious notion. Just the same, it was a relief when the uncanny silence was shattered by a noisy flapping of wings and a hoarse cackle as a cock pheasant lifted almost vertically from behind a nearby tussock of grass. A flock of rooks appeared, black against the limpid sky, splintering the air with their raucous cries. Smaller birds came fluttering down to peck at the nuts and seeds on the feeding table in Melissa's garden. Reassured by these signs of normality, she got into her car and set off for town.

Ken Harris had left Hawthorn Cottage at sunrise, giving as his excuse for such an early departure his need to go home for a shave and a clean shirt, but Melissa knew that the real reason was an old-fashioned regard for her reputation. Amused by the thought, she had pointed out that the Fords were the only couple in the neighbourhood who considered an affair between free adults a cause for gossip, and that since they lived at the other end of the village they were unlikely to be aware of the latest development. In any case, the murder, once it became known, would sweep all other topics into oblivion for days to come. Harris, however, had been adamant.

They had agreed to meet later and go together to police headquarters to make the formal statements that Acting Chief Inspector Holloway had requested. As a result, shortly before half-past ten on Monday morning, Melissa parked the Golf in the multi-storey car park and went to the machine to buy a ticket. As she put her coin in the slot, she became aware of a woman's voice raised in anger. For a moment she thought it was an argument over a parking space; glancing round, she saw the speaker shaking her fist in the direction of a new and expensive car parked a short distance away. There was a fierce revving as the engine started up; above it, the shouting continued, shrill and querulous, breaking into words that echoed off the concrete walls.

'Think yourself so clever, don't you Daisy Grice, with your smart clothes and your fancy car! I'll bet your posh friends don't know how you used to earn your money!'

Beside herself with rage, the woman ran forward and

hammered with gloved fists on the boot of the car, then leapt aside as the driver began reversing out. Melissa caught a brief glimpse of dark hair, a finely chiselled feminine profile and red lips compressed in a hard line, before the car swung round and sped away. The first woman stood glaring after it for a moment, breathing heavily and muttering under her breath, before turning on her heel and marching towards the lift. On seeing Melissa she stopped short and put a hand to her mouth, evidently startled at realising that there had been a witness to her outburst. Then her anger took control again.

'Did you see that?' she panted, swinging round and gesturing with a theatrical sweep of one hand. 'Looks at me as if I was dirt beneath her feet. If it hadn't been for me, she'd still be in the gutter. I greet her as an old friend – which I was, and believe me, she never had a better – and the bitch cuts me dead. Well, I'll show her. I'll find out where she lives . . . I'll let her know she can't do that to Laura Maddox and get away with it.' The words rushed out in a vitriolic flood as she watched the car disappearing down the ramp towards the exit.

She was about Melissa's own age, handsome in a hard, flamboyant fashion, with a voluptuously rounded figure and a sensual mouth. She was carefully groomed and made up, her blond hair simply but elegantly styled. Her blue woollen coat was plain but well cut and she was generously annointed with good quality perfume.

On the final words, she had turned to look Melissa full in the face, as if seeking support for her justifiable grievance. Intrigued by the incident, her writer's curiosity aroused, Melissa temporarily forgot her rendezvous with Ken Harris.

'It often happens, doesn't it?' she agreed. 'When people

go up in the world, they don't always want to know their old friends.'

'. . . know their old friends,' echoed the woman. 'She needn't think she's heard the last of me, though . . . I'll find her . . . I'll show her up . . . her and her fancy notions . . .'

'Fancy notions?' prompted Melissa as Laura Maddox showed signs of running out of steam.

'Fancy notions,' Laura repeated, and was off again. 'Always lived in a dream world, she did. Bastard daughter of a junkie who died of an overdose, that's all she was when I met her, but to hear her talk, you'd think she was of the blood royal. My Dad and me, we take her in, give her a job, look after her . . . then she takes up with a rich man – that *we* introduced her to, would you believe – and starts putting on airs, doesn't want to know her old friends, oh no! How's that for gratitude?'

It occurred to Melissa that, judging by her appearance, Laura Maddox hadn't done too badly either. However, some further sympathetic comment was obviously expected.

'That was a bit unkind of her,' she agreed.

'. . . unkind of her,' said Laura. 'You can say that again,' she added with unconscious humour before consulting an expensive-looking wrist-watch. 'Oh, goodness, look at the time. I was supposed to meet my Cliffie half an hour ago. Poor darling, he'll be so worried.' Her manner had altered completely, becoming almost arch as she put a hand on Melissa's arm and whispered, 'These young men get in a panic so easily, don't they?'

This time, Melissa found herself at a loss for an appropriate comment, but none seemed expected. Her ill temper apparently forgotten, Laura gave a gracious smile, purred, 'Goodbye, it's been so nice talking to you,' and headed for the lift.

Melissa fixed her ticket to her windscreen, locked the car and made her way to the office of Harris Investigations, where she found the proprietor and his assistant in earnest, and apparently puzzled, consultation.

'Something wrong?' she asked.

'Just the person we need,' said Harris. 'Guess who wants to talk to you.'

'No idea.'

'Mrs Aggs.'

'What on earth does Mrs Aggs want with me?'

'She wouldn't say. Apparently, when she saw you here on Friday, she half recognised you but couldn't place you. Then she saw you being interviewed in the *Crime Pays* book programme that evening and she was on the phone as soon as the office opened.'

'I still don't understand . . .'

'Neither do we, but she begged to be put in touch with you. She sounded a bit . . . how did you describe it, Trish? Not agitated . . .'

'Intense,' said Tricia. 'With a hint of high drama. She was at pains to assure me that she's a fan of your books, but it isn't your writing she wants to talk about. She kept on about something *very delicate*, but she flatly refused to go into details.'

'How odd,' commented Melissa. 'Well, I'll think about it.' She turned to Harris. 'Are we going to get this statement business over?'

'Sure. Back in about an hour, Trish.'

It was a relief to learn, on reaching police headquarters, that Acting DCI Holloway was out. They made their statements to Sergeant Matthew Waters, with whom ex-DCI Harris had worked for many years. When they had finished, there was a suggestion that the two men meet for a drink that evening, but when Melissa intervened with an invitation to them both for supper, it was accepted with alacrity.

On the way back to the office, Harris said, 'Sorry, I forgot when I suggested meeting Matt this evening that you'd be needing company again.'

The implication was obvious and she hastened to put the record straight. 'It wasn't so much that . . .' she began.

They pulled up at some traffic lights; he took a hand off the wheel, put it on her knee and gave a proprietary squeeze. 'I'll stay for as long as you need me,' he said.

Feeling as if her life was suddenly at a crossroads, she said, 'I'll be okay on my own tonight.'

'Are you sure?' He sounded disappointed.

'It's a bit like driving again after an accident, isn't it – the sooner the better. I have to face up to it some time.'

'Not necessarily.' The words were spoken deliberately, charged with unmistakable meaning.

'Ken, let's not talk about that now.'

He gave a resigned sigh. 'Oh, all right.' He swung the car into the reserved space behind the converted Regency building that housed his office. 'What about Mrs Aggs? Are you going to give her a call?'

'I'm not sure I want to. From what you told me, I've a feeling she intends to use me as a sort of agony aunt. If that's all she needs, there are professionals she could go to.'

'It wouldn't do any harm to find out what's on her mind. You can always say no.'

She turned to face him. 'Why this sudden interest in Mrs Aggs?'

He shrugged, but did not meet her eye. 'Just curious. Aren't you?'

'I'm not exactly burning to know, but – oh, very well. Shall I do it from here?'

'Of course. Use the phone in my office – I'd like to listen in.'

'You've got a hunch about this, haven't you?'

'Just curious,' he repeated non-committally.

She knew from experience that he would say nothing more for the moment. They went upstairs to his office and she tapped out the number Tricia gave her. It rang for several seconds; she was on the point of hanging up when a woman's voice came on the line.

'Thanebury 510364.'

'Is that Mrs Aggs?'

'Yes.' The tone was guarded, almost suspicious. 'Who's calling?'

'This is Mel Craig. I understand you want to speak to me.'

'Oh, Ms Craig, you got my message.' The tension in the voice disappeared and words came tumbling out in a rush. 'I saw you leaving the office of that private detective last Friday and I said to myself, I know I've seen her before, but I couldn't remember exactly who you were . . . you know how it is . . . and then I saw you on the television on Saturday . . .'

'Yes, Miss Jessop explained,' Melissa broke in, trying not to sound impatient. 'What can I do for you, Mrs Aggs?'

'Ms Craig, could we possibly meet somewhere? I'd very much like to talk to you.'

'What about?'

'I'd really rather not say on the phone. It's . . . very delicate. I think you may be able to help me . . . perhaps advise me.' The voice became less confident, breaking off on a rising note of anxiety.

It was on the tip of Melissa's tongue to enquire if the matter had anything to do with the woman's suspicions regarding her husband's nocturnal excursions, but held back. It would not do for the proprietor of Harris Investigations to acquire a reputation for betraying client confidentiality. So she said, hoping to coax Mrs Aggs into being a little more forthcoming, 'It's a little unusual. Perhaps if you wrote to me . . .'

'No, I couldn't possibly put anything in writing. Please, Ms Craig, I won't take up too much of your time. I must talk to someone and I think perhaps you . . . I know from your books that you understand how . . . how people's minds work . . . certain people, that is . . . what makes them do the things they do . . .'

Across the desk, Melissa mouthed, 'What do you think?' and Harris mouthed back, 'Say yes.'

'All right, Mrs Aggs,' she said into the phone. 'I'm in Cheltenham now. Suppose we meet somewhere for lunch? How about . . .' Before she could suggest a venue, she was interrupted.

'Not a restaurant,' said Mrs Aggs hurriedly, 'it's too public. Someone might overhear . . . how about the multi-storey car park? We can talk in my car.'

'That'd be fine – I'm already parked there as it happens, on level four.' Melissa glanced at her watch. 'Can you be there by twelve o'clock? My ticket expires at half-past.'

'Oh yes, quite easily. Thank you *so* much.'

The relief in the woman's voice was so strong that for

a moment Melissa thought she was going to break down, but she controlled herself, cleared her throat and gave a description of her car and its registration number before repeating profuse thanks and ringing off.

'What do you make of that?' Melissa said as she hung up.

'That she suspects her husband of something other than having an affair,' Harris replied without hesitation.

'Such as what?'

'I thought perhaps you could find out. You suggested the other day that I take you on as a partner. Right, here's your chance . . . strictly on a trial basis, of course.' The grin that creased his lumpy features was provocative.

'You've got a nerve! I remember times when you positively forbade me to poke my nose into your cases.'

The grin broadened. 'Never took much notice, did you?'

Melissa ignored the jibe. 'I'm leaving,' she announced. 'I'll give you a call if I unearth anything sensational. Otherwise, I'll expect you and Matt Waters about seven. Thank you, I'll see myself out,' she added sarcastically as he made a half-hearted effort to reach the door ahead of her.

With twenty minutes to spare, she browsed for a while among the new season's fashions in Cavendish House. At a few minutes to twelve, she made her way back to the car park. As she stepped out of the lift on level four, a light green Metro appeared. There was a brief flash of headlights before the driver swung the car into an empty space and cut the engine.

As she went to keep her appointment with Mrs Aggs, she thought back briefly to her extraordinary encounter with Laura Maddox and made a mental note to jot down some details when she got home. It was the kind of episode that might one day develop into a plot. A fictitious plot, naturally.

Chapter Five

Mrs Aggs reached across to unlock the passenger door and beckoned Melissa to get into the car beside her.

'I don't want anyone I know to see me with you . . . they might start asking questions, or say something to Raymond . . . my husband.' Her expression was a mixture of embarrassment and anxiety. 'It's very good of you to come, Mrs Craig. It must seem very odd, my asking you to meet me like this.'

'Don't worry about it.' Melissa did her best to sound reassuring. She was on the point of proposing that they use first names as an ice-breaker, but decided against it. Something about the woman's demeanour suggested that even now, after having taken the unusual step of seeking to confide a delicate personal problem to a stranger, she might see any move towards intimacy as a subtle attempt to woo her into saying more than she intended. She was evidently under considerable strain, for she sat bolt upright in the driving seat, staring through the windscreen at the concrete and steel barrier, biting her lips and fidgeting with the steering-wheel. At last, without turning to look at Melissa, she said, 'Are you married?'

The unexpected question brought back some poignant memories for Melissa. She and Guy, her first love, had had little time to speak of marriage; their passionate youthful affair had ended in tragedy with his death in a road accident. The one stipulation that his parents had made when they took her in, grief-stricken, five months pregnant and rejected by her own father and mother, was that she should wear a wedding ring, change her name to theirs and pass it on to his son.

All this was hardly relevant, and in any case not something she normally confided to total strangers, so she replied simply, 'My husband died many years ago.'

Mrs Aggs turned to look directly at her for the first time. Beneath the unbecoming hat which Ken Harris had so graphically described, her homely features had a haggard look and there was a puffiness about her light brown, slightly bloodshot eyes which hinted at a lack of sleep. But her voice, which up to now had sounded harsh and brittle, softened as she said, 'I'm so sorry.'

'Thank you.'

'At least, you have some experience of what marriage is about.'

Unwilling to be led along that path, Melissa made a slight movement with her hands and waited. Eventually, Mrs Aggs went on, 'If *your* husband started going off in the middle of the night, fully dressed, staying out an hour or more, what would you do?'

'I'd ask him where he'd been, naturally.'

'Suppose you weren't satisfied with what he told you?'

'Then I'd question him a little more closely.'

'And if he still persisted with a story that you were convinced was untrue?'

Melissa hesitated for a moment before saying gently, 'Mrs Aggs, please stop beating about the bush. Do you suspect your husband of having an affair?'

This time, the silence was longer. Mrs Aggs once more stared straight ahead, breathing heavily. Her face was set in an expression of grim determination, but a twitching muscle at the corner of her pale, unpainted mouth betrayed a latent agitation. The hands that had moved restlessly on the wheel now gripped it so fiercely that the knuckles threatened to split the thin leather gloves. She was very near snapping point.

'I wish it was as simple as that,' she said in a voice as taut as piano wire.

There was another pause. This time, Melissa ended it by saying, 'Mrs Aggs, you referred on the telephone to what you described as my understanding of what makes people do the things they do. I take it you meant when their actions seem out of character.'

Mrs Aggs nodded and said hesitantly, 'You've written about people . . . some of them good, respectable, God-fearing people . . . who suddenly commit terrible deeds . . . but sometimes their motives aren't always evil . . . not to them, at any rate.'

'Yes, I suppose that's true,' Melissa agreed, wondering what on earth was coming next.

'That can happen in real life as well, can't it?'

'Mrs Aggs, what is it you're trying to tell me? Are you afraid your husband has committed a crime? Is that what you're saying?'

Mrs Aggs nodded, her mouth working as she fought to hold back tears. Melissa put a hand on her arm and asked gently, 'Can you tell me what you think it is?'

'Something terrible.' The woman took several deep, shuddering breaths and then, her face half averted, whispered, 'I think . . . I'm afraid . . . he may have committed murder.'

'Murder?' Melissa felt her jaw drop in astonishment. During the conversation, various possibilities had been running through her head. With a wife as frankly lacking in sex appeal as Mrs Aggs, a man might well seek entertainment elsewhere, not necessarily with a regular mistress. Kerb crawler, flasher, transvestite – to think one's husband capable of being any of these would cause understandable distress to a wife, particularly one as inhibited as Mrs Aggs appeared to be. But to suspect him of murder every time he left the house without a satisfactory explanation seemed an over-reaction, to say the least. Melissa began to wish she had never agreed to the meeting.

Aloud, she said, 'Who do you suspect him of murdering?'

As if she had not heard the question, Mrs Aggs began speaking again, in clipped, muttered sentences that Melissa had to strain to hear.

'I know it's wicked of me . . . I keep telling myself how wicked I am . . . but I can't help it.' In her anguish, she tugged convulsively at the wheel as if she was trying to shake it loose. 'I had to tell someone . . . I went to see Mr Harris . . . that private detective . . . but I couldn't bring myself to . . . I pretended . . . I made up . . . I wanted Raymond watched . . . I hadn't realised it would cost so much . . .' The words streamed out as if a dam had been split apart. Feeling utterly helpless, Melissa could only wait in silence until the flow subsided.

'You must have heard,' Mrs Aggs went on, after a pause during which she was plainly struggling not to break down altogether. 'It's been in all the local papers . . . three elderly people in the Thanebury area . . . one after the other . . . found suffocated in their beds.'

The temperature inside the car had been dropping steadily, but in her thick winter coat, Melissa had until that moment been barely conscious of the fact. Now it seemed as if the cold had entered her bones and drained every vestige of warmth from her body. Was it possible that the woman sitting beside her was the wife of the perverted killer who only two nights ago had claimed his fourth victim? At the memory of the dreadful, painted smile on the dead face of Martha Willis, she gave an involuntary gasp and put a hand to her mouth.

Meanwhile, Mrs Aggs was stumbling on. 'Looking back, I think . . . I'm almost sure at least two of them were killed about the times when Raymond . . .' Her voice, becoming progressively weaker, failed altogether, as if even now she could not bring herself to put into words the fear that had tormented her for so long.

Melissa, her attention distracted by her own thoughts and for the moment too startled to speak, suddenly felt a hand on her arm. She turned to see Mrs Aggs looking at her with an expression of concern on her face.

'I'm so sorry . . . I've shocked you . . . I didn't mean to. It was very inconsiderate of me to come out with it like that.'

'Oh please, don't apologise. It's just . . . you couldn't possibly have known . . .'

'Known what?'

'Did your husband go out on Saturday night?'

'The night before last, do you mean?' Melissa nodded. 'No, I'm sure he didn't. Why do you ask?'

'Then I think I can put your mind at rest. You see, yesterday afternoon, a woman in my village was suffocated in her bed . . . in fact, I was the one who found her.'

'Oh my goodness, how dreadful for you. But . . . yesterday afternoon?' For a moment, Mrs Aggs appeared unable to grasp the significance of what she had just heard.

'The doctor who examined the body was sure she had been killed some time during Saturday night,' Melissa explained.

For a moment or two, Mrs Aggs was silent. Then she asked in a low voice, 'Was there anything . . . unusual about the body?'

'What do you mean by "unusual"?'

Mrs Aggs seemed to find the question disconcerting. She hesitated again before saying hurriedly, 'I mean, anything to connect the lady's death with those others?'

'The police have asked me not to discuss details of the case with anyone,' Melissa replied cautiously.

'Yes, of course, I quite understand . . . but you do see, don't you, if she was killed by the same person . . .' Mrs Aggs' voice became steadier and her speech more rapid as her hopes began rising. 'Raymond hasn't been out at night since poor Miss Twigg was murdered – and her body wasn't discovered for several days and the police weren't exactly sure when it happened – so in that case . . .'

'I understand the police are working on the theory that Miss Willis was a victim of the same serial killer who . . .'

Before Melissa could finish the sentence, Mrs Aggs gave a harsh cry of, 'Oh, thank God!' and burst into a spasm of hysterical weeping. She collapsed over the wheel and sobbed, her shoulders heaving as the pent-up fears of many weeks rushed out on a tidal wave of relief. When at last she became calmer, she fumbled in her handbag, pulled out a handkerchief and dried her eyes.

'Please forgive me for making such an exhibition of myself,' she faltered. She blew her nose and put away the handkerchief. 'I feel so foolish . . . what must you think of me?'

'It's a perfectly normal reaction after being under so much stress.'

'However could I have imagined that Raymond, of all men, was capable of such dreadful deeds?'

'We all get wrong ideas about people sometimes.'

'But my own husband, a devout churchgoer . . . oh, how wicked I've been! What can I do to make it up to him? I know, I'll cook him his favourite supper tonight . . . grilled steak . . . he loves that.'

The change in the woman's manner was so comical, bordering on the ludicrous, that Melissa could not help laughing aloud. 'I wouldn't overdo it or he'll think *you've* been up to something,' she advised.

'What? Oh, I see what you mean?' Mrs Aggs put a hand to her mouth and gave an almost girlish titter. 'Really, Mrs Craig, you are naughty!'

She was, Melissa reflected, as unsophisticated as she was neurotic – a combination which could well account for her husband's occasional nocturnal escapades. That, and her unfortunate choice of hats . . . deciding that it was time to close this extraordinary interview, she opened the car door and said, 'I'll be getting along now, if you don't mind.'

'Mrs Craig, I can't thank you enough for . . .'

'I'm glad I was able to help . . . goodbye.'

How ironic, she thought as she made her way back to her own car, that the death of one elderly woman could bring such solace to a total stranger. She opened her driver's door and was in the act of getting in, still mulling over the encounter, when she became aware of voices close at hand. One was that of a man, strong, resonant, young-sounding, with a local accent. The other was a woman's, a little husky, the accent suggesting London or the Home Counties – a voice that Melissa had heard before.

'You've got enough here to stock a canteen,' the man was saying. There was a faint thud, suggesting that a heavy package had been deposited in a car boot.

Laura Maddox gave a throaty chuckle. 'I'll bet they don't serve *this* kind of food in the police canteen!'

'Hardly,' he agreed. There was a second thud, and then a third, accompanied by a chink of glass. 'Is that it?'

'That's it for now, my pet. Laura likes to keep her larder well stocked for her favourite little copper.'

'You're an angel!' A maudlin note crept into the manly tenor. 'When will I see you again?'

'When you've done what Laura asked you, sweetie-pie.'

'Not till then?' He sounded dismayed.

'Not till then. Then,' – the voice became wheedling, babyish, sensuous – 'Laura will give her Cliffie anything he wants.'

'But it could be days before I get the chance to . . .' He dropped his voice so that Melissa, unashamedly listening through her half-open door, could no longer hear what he was saying. So the 'poor darling' who was liable to panic if his lady-love was half an hour late was a policeman; that was interesting. She wondered if any of his brother officers or, more significantly, his superiors knew that he was heavily involved with a woman at least twice his age.

There came the sound of a boot lid being slammed

down, then silence. Curiosity got the better of Melissa; she put one foot on the ground and cautiously raised herself until she could see across the two intervening cars. The couple were in the act of slowly detaching themselves from a passionate embrace. Melissa hastily sat down again.

There were a few more whispered words, then a door slammed and an engine started up. Laura's car reversed out and drove away; Clifford stood waving after it for several seconds and then turned and walked back towards the pedestrian exit, passing within a few feet of Melissa's car but obviously unaware of her presence. He was clean-shaven with regular, slightly tanned features, tall, slim but well built, and moved with an athletic stride. Just the sort of young demi-god to arouse the passion of an over-sexed older woman.

Melissa watched him disappear with a feeling of almost maternal concern. She'd seen it happen before, to one of her son's college friends. When the woman had ditched him for a new plaything, he had turned to drink and flunked his exams. Part of her wanted to run after 'Cliffie' and warn him, but she dismissed the notion out of hand. He was a total stranger and his problems were no concern of hers.

Or so she believed at the time.

Chapter Six

On the way home, Melissa called in at the village shop. Several customers, their expressions varying from stunned bewilderment to an overtly morbid interest, pounced on her as she entered and plied her with questions: was it true that she was the one who found the body? Was it really murder? Had the victim been, er, – here the questioner's voice dropped to a prurient whisper – *interfered with*? Do the police have any clues? What kind of monster would kill a harmless old woman like Martha Willis?

A further question lurked in their eyes but remained unspoken, as if to put it into words would in some inexplicable way bring the horror closer: will he strike amongst us again, and if so, who will be the next victim?

Doing her best to satisfy their curiosity without revealing details the police wished kept secret, Melissa found herself once more reliving the moment of her grim discovery, seeing yet again the staring eyes and the ghastly, painted grimace on the discoloured features. Her agitation must have shown, for Alice Hamley said quickly, 'I don't think we should bother Mrs Craig with too many questions. I'm sure finding Miss Willis was a dreadful shock to her.'

'It was, rather,' Melissa agreed. More to gain time to pull herself together than to refresh her memory, she consulted the shopping list she had hastily scribbled on the back of an envelope before leaving the car park.

Alice's mild reproof induced a brief silence before curiosity overcame discretion. 'How d'you suppose the murderer got in?' someone asked.

'I think she must have forgotten to lock her back door,' said Melissa. 'The key was on the inside.'

'There, that's what I said might have happened,' declared Mrs Foster with a note of macabre satisfaction in her voice. 'Didn't I say, I wouldn't be surprised if she left her door unlocked?' Her pale eyes, fringed with colourless lashes, flickered round the group. Heads nodded in confirmation. 'Major Ford was always telling her to be more careful, but she just laughed,' she went on. '"Who's going to rob me?" she'd say. "I've nothing worth stealing." And I'll tell you something else,' Mrs Foster leaned across the counter and wagged a plump forefinger at the circle of faces. 'She used to leave a spare key under a flower pot, so's anyone could get in if she were taken bad, like. That used to worry her quite a lot, that did. She were getting pretty frail . . .'

'She'd been much happier since the Donovans moved into Larkfield Barn,' Alice pointed out. 'Those girls have been so good to her, popping in for a chat, fetching her shopping, getting her prescriptions made up . . .'

'That reminds me,' said Melissa. 'I should call in and see them. Sirry telephoned me as soon as she heard the news, but I was too shaken to talk to her.'

'Aaah!' A somewhat belated wave of sympathy undulated round the shop. Mrs Foster, a knowing expression on her round pink face, added, as if by way of consolation,

'Still, I suppose in your line of work, you get used to dealing with dead bodies and such.'

'Not real ones.' Despite the seriousness of the situation, Melissa found it difficult not to smile at this pragmatic attitude to murder. 'Killing people off in books doesn't really prepare one for the real thing.'

'Of course it doesn't,' said Alice. 'It's a terrible thing to happen in the village. John and I were dreadfully shocked when we heard about it. Tell me, Melissa, is it really true the police are looking for a serial killer?'

'I'm sure they're considering all manner of possibilities,' said Melissa cautiously. 'I expect there'll be a statement on the news this evening. We might learn something more definite then.'

'No doubt we'll be hearing Major Ford's views on the subject,' said Mrs Foster tartly. 'Soon as he heard there were reporters here, he couldn't get up to Miss Willis's cottage quick enough.'

Melissa's heart sank. With his uncanny skill at extracting information from even the most reticent, Dudley Ford would almost certainly have uncovered details of her own rôle in the case and passed it on to the media. There would probably be a posse of journalists and TV reporters lying in wait for her when she reached home. For a moment she toyed with the idea of leaving the car and returning on foot via a path leading past the church; it might just be possible to sneak along the bank behind Hawthorn Cottage and in at her back door without being observed. She quickly abandoned the idea; with the tenacity of their kind, the ratpack would simply hang around for as long as it took. They would still be there when Ken Harris and Matt Waters arrived and that would really give them something to get their teeth into. The only sensible course was to go straight home, face them, answer their questions and let them take a few mug shots. That way, with any luck, they'd pack up and leave her in peace.

Resignedly, she began selecting fruit and vegetables from the self-service display. The other customers appeared to accept this as a sign that the discussion was over and one by one took their leave.

When Melissa left the shop she found Alice waiting outside. 'I've been wondering,' she said, 'whether you could spare a few minutes to tell John a bit about Miss Willis's background . . . how long she lived in the village and so on. She doesn't seem to have had any close relatives. John'll be giving the funeral address, and as we've been in the parish only a short time . . .'

'I'd be glad to,' said Melissa, 'although there are plenty of people who've lived here longer than I have.'

'Oh yes, but I'm sure you know all the village history. And of course,' Alice added earnestly, 'if you think it would relieve your mind to talk about your dreadful experience, John's a trained counsellor and I'm sure he'd be able to . . . I mean, it can be so helpful in dealing with trauma, talking to someone who understands the effect it can have on the mind.'

'Oh, I'm sure it can, if one feels the need,' Melissa replied politely, while thinking that, not so long ago, one simply relied on family, friends and neighbours for comfort and support in times of trouble. Nowadays one was said to be traumatised and in need of professional counselling. Still, there was no doubting Alice's utter sincerity. A slim figure in jeans and a denim jacket, a woollen cap on her fine blond hair, she studied Melissa's face with genuine concern in her clear blue eyes.

'I thought perhaps you might like to come and have

coffee with us tomorrow morning,' she went on before Melissa could say a word. 'John will be at home then.'

'It's very kind of you, but really . . .'

'Say about eleven o'clock?'

'Well, thank you.'

'We'll look forward to seeing you. And of course, if you feel the need to talk to someone in the meantime . . .'

'I'll be all right, really. I have some friends coming to supper this evening.'

'Oh, I'm *so* glad. It's not good to be alone at times like this.' As if a burden had been lifted from her shoulders, Alice picked up her shopping bag, which she had deposited on the ground while waiting for Melissa. 'Well, I must run along. I've got several things to see to before the children come home from school. See you tomorrow.' She set off for the rectory on foot and Melissa drove the short distance home.

Several cars were parked in the lane beyond the track leading to Hawthorn and Elder Cottages. As soon as they spotted the Golf, the occupants leapt out and raced after it, closing in behind as if anticipating an attempt to evade them. They clustered round Melissa, waving furry microphones and pointing cameras while firing off questions, most of them on similar lines to the ones her neighbours had been putting to her minutes before. There was, however, less reticence on the subject of possible future attacks.

'There are several people living alone in the village,' she admitted, 'but I'm certainly not going to name any of them. No,' – in response to a supplementary question – 'I don't see myself as a potential victim.'

'Perhaps you see this series of murders as a possible

idea for a new crime novel?' suggested a bespectacled woman with a notebook.

'Series of murders?' Melissa repeated guardedly.

'This and the three in the Thanebury area. They've all been committed by the same person, haven't they?'

'That hasn't been established, so far as I know . . . and I never base my novels on actual crimes. Now, if you'll excuse me, I've already answered a lot of questions today.'

A young female photographer stepped forward and said, 'Just a couple of pictures, if you don't mind. By your front door . . . that's lovely.' The shutter clicked several times and the girl thanked her and walked away. Relieved at being let off the hook, Melissa turned to put her key in the front door, but a middle-aged man in a shabby anorak suddenly thrust a microphone under her nose.

'Before you go in,' he said with a disarming smile. 'I do have one more question.'

'Yes?'

'Can you tell us if there was anything at all unusual or unnatural about the appearance of the deceased?'

The entire group had fallen silent, awaiting her reply. Melissa had the impression that the man was speaking on behalf of all of them. She recalled a newspaper report on the Thanebury murders, referring to 'a wall of silence' among the shocked inhabitants. The press obviously knew, or strongly suspected, that some vital piece of information was being withheld from them and the public at large, but no one would speak of it. This group had probably agreed in advance that one of their number would slip in a leading question at the end of the interview, hoping to catch her off guard. Well, she thought, with a certain malicious glee, she had enough experience to fend off the occasional googly.

'The fact that she was deceased struck me as unusual,' she said drily. 'And, not being one of my fictitious sleuths, I didn't stop to make a detailed examination.'

'So how could you be sure she was dead?' persisted the shabby anorak.

'I wasn't a hundred per cent sure – I'm not a doctor – but I could tell there was something seriously wrong.'

'So there *was* something unnatural about her appearance?'

'Of course there was. Her eyes were staring and she was blue in the face. I shouted for my friend who was waiting outside. He had his mobile phone with him and he took charge from then on.'

'That'd be ex-DCI Harris, the proprietor of Harris Investigations,' said the girl with the notebook, scribbling furiously. It was a comment, not a question.

Damn you and your big mouth, Dudley Ford. This mob'll be at Ken's door next. Aloud, Melissa said firmly, 'There's nothing more I can tell you, I'm afraid. No doubt the police will be issuing further statements in due course.' And this time, resigned to defeat, the representatives of the fourth estate departed.

Melissa had eaten very little for over twenty-four hours and was beginning to feel empty. She made sandwiches, brewed a pot of tea and carried a tray up to her study, where she noticed that the light on her answering machine was flashing. Thinking Ken Harris might have called to find out if Mrs Aggs had said anything of interest, she played back the message. It was from Sirry, asking if there was any further news about Martha's killer. It had already crossed her mind to go and see the Donovans, and when she had finished her lunch she put on her coat and set off on the short walk to Larkfield Barn.

The way took her past Martha Willis's cottage, still sealed off with blue and white tape. A uniformed policeman stood at the gate and a small knot of bystanders had gathered in a convenient field entrance to stare, nudge one another and take photographs. All were strangers. One man, his face alight with ghoulish curiosity, tried to waylay Melissa, asking if she lived in the village and whether she had known the deceased, but she cut him short with a curt, 'I've nothing to say,' and was conscious of resentful eyes following her as she passed.

Genty Donovan opened the front door in response to Melissa's ring. Her expression, half wary, half apprehensive, softened into relief as she recognised her visitor.

'Oh Melissa, thank you so much for calling. Do come in. Sirry, it's Melissa,' she called over her shoulder and her elder sister appeared through a door at the back of the small entrance hall. Neither woman wore make-up and both looked pale and strained. They led the way into a sitting-room with mullioned windows, a great deal of exposed brickwork and wooden beams, and a log fire burning on a stone hearth. There was plenty of comfortable-looking, chintz-covered furniture, and colourful rugs on the polished wooden floor, but few ornaments of any kind and none of the conventional copper and brass knick-knacks so often found in similar dwellings. There were, however, several landscapes in oils hanging on the walls and over the fireplace was a portrait of a young man with a strong resemblance to Cluny Donovan.

'Our brother, Saxe,' said Genty softly as she saw Melissa's eyes on it. 'There are several portraits of him in different parts of the house. Father likes to feel he's still with us. We all do, of course.' Her voice dropped to a whisper and both sisters stood for a moment, one on either side of their visitor, looking up at the portrait in silence. There was something reverent about their attitude; their hands were clasped in front of them as if they were praying before an altar. Then they turned to her with welcoming smiles and invited her to sit down, and the illusion vanished.

'It's been dreadful here this morning,' said Sirry. 'First the police, then the reporters.'

'It wasn't as if we could tell them anything,' Genty complained. 'The policeman who called here asked us a lot of questions, but he wouldn't answer any of ours.'

'That's the way they work,' Melissa explained. 'I suppose they wanted to know when you last saw Martha and if you noticed anyone hanging around acting suspiciously, that sort of thing? That's routine . . . making house-to-house enquiries. Did the officer speak to your father?'

'Oh no!' the sisters exclaimed in a shocked chorus.

'We told him that it would distress Father too much,' said Sirry. 'And anyway, he hardly ever goes out and if he saw anyone passing he wouldn't know who was a stranger and who lived in the village.'

'Oh well, I daresay they won't bother you again,' said Melissa. 'I'm afraid I can't tell you any more than you know already, but if I do hear anything, of course I'll let you know. Did the reporters make nuisances of themselves?'

'Not really,' said Genty. 'We just told them we'd only lived here a little while, and they took one or two photos and went away. It was you they wanted to talk to – I believe Major Ford told them you found Martha's body.'

'I rather thought so,' said Melissa grimly. 'That man can't keep his mouth shut about anything.'

'For once, we've been thankful Father is having one of his reclusive days,' said Sirry. 'He's been sitting in his studio ever since breakfast, staring at Saxe's portrait. We haven't even told him Martha is dead.'

'He must be a great anxiety to you,' said Melissa. The remark sounded trite and inadequate, but for the moment she was unable to think of anything more constructive to say. The sisters sat side by side on the settee, their hands folded in their laps, their expressions solemn. There was a slightly foreign air about them; the high cheekbones and sensuous mouths inherited from their Polish mother gave them an air of brooding intensity. In response to Melissa's remark they sighed and nodded in agreement.

'Every day we hope he will start work again, but so far, nothing.' Genty shrugged her shoulders and spread her hands. The gesture, too, had something foreign about it.

'We mustn't burden Melissa with our problems,' Sirry interposed.

'No, of course we mustn't,' Genty agreed. In a barely discernible movement, the sisters edged closer together until their shoulders were touching, their sombre eyes fixed on their visitor. They seemed to be signalling that they wished the interview to be brought to an end.

Melissa got to her feet. 'I'd better be getting home,' she said briskly. 'I've got some people coming for supper.'

Back home, she spent a short time in her study writing a brief account of her conversation with Mrs Aggs and the bizarre behaviour of Laura Maddox. One never knew when such odd encounters might be used as a twist in some future plot.

It did not enter her head, as she closed her notebook and went downstairs to begin preparations for the evening meal, that each of the morning's apparently unconnected events was part of an increasingly complex web in which she would shortly become enmeshed, with chilling consequences.

Chapter Seven

'So what did old Mother Aggs have on her mind?' asked Ken Harris between mouthfuls of beef goulash.

'If you mean *Mrs* Aggs . . .' Melissa said pointedly.

'Sorry, *Mrs* Aggs,' Harris repeated in a tone of mock contrition. He winked at Matt Waters, seated beside him at the table in the dining-room of Hawthorn Cottage, and said in an exaggerated stage whisper, 'Have to humour these touchy ladies, y'know, or they'll be after us for sexual harassment!' The pair exchanged old-boy grins before turning blandly innocent faces to their hostess.

'Wonderful goulash!' enthused Waters.

'Superb!' agreed Harris before engulfing another forkful.

'Never mind the flannel,' Melissa scolded them. 'I never hear comments about "old *Father* So-and-so", but when it's a woman you're speaking of . . .'

'And an old hatchet-face to boot,' Harris informed Waters.

'Mrs Aggs can't help her looks, and you're no oil-painting yourself,' Melissa retorted.

'Got you there!' Waters grinned at his former chief.

'I don't deny it. I'm the original ugly duckling that never made it to a swan.' A slow smile spread over Harris's lumpy features and, as always, Melissa felt herself melting. 'Come on, Mel,' he coaxed, 'quit stalling. Why was *Mrs* Aggs so frantic to talk to you?'

'In case you hadn't noticed, she was a very worried lady, and if you'd shown a little more sympathy she might have confided in you and you might still have a client . . . or rather . . . no, as it happens, you wouldn't, not any more.'

'Meaning?'

'Meaning I was able to put her mind at rest.'

'So what exactly . . . ?'

'Before I answer that, perhaps you wouldn't mind explaining why you were so anxious for me to see her.'

Harris demolished the last of his second helping of goulash and laid down his fork. 'A wild idea came into my head, a sort of hunch . . .'

'Yes?'

'I was obviously on the wrong track, or you'd have been on the phone straight away, but I remembered that she lives in Thanebury, and Mr Aggs has been sneaking out in the small hours, like the Smiler.'

'Like the what?'

'The psycho who's been committing all these killings,' Waters explained. 'We call him the Smiler because . . .'

'Thanks, I get the point,' Melissa said hastily. She turned back to Harris. 'So you thought Mrs Aggs suspected her husband. You might have told me.'

'I didn't want you to have any preconceptions,' he explained. 'Like I said, it seemed a wild idea, but when she begged to be put in touch with you, I thought it would be interesting to see what she had to say. Sorry if it was a waste of your time.'

'Oh, it wasn't a waste of time, on the contrary. As I told you, I was able to put the poor woman's mind completely at rest. She actually broke down and wept with relief.'

'How very touching. Now, just to satisfy our curiosity, will you please tell us what it was all about?'

'Us?' Melissa looked accusingly from one to the other as she handed round servings of blackberry and apple pie and cream. 'You two were in cahoots over this?'

'Well . . .' The police sergeant and the retired chief inspector exchanged sheepish glances.

'We'd better come clean,' said Waters. 'It's like this, Mel. We're getting pretty frustrated over these Thanebury killings and the fact that the Smiler appears to have struck further afield has opened up a whole new ball-game. We haven't had a single lead worth the name, but Ken told us about Mrs Aggs and how she happened to come from Thanebury. Something was bugging her, she couldn't bring herself to tell Ken so the odds were she wouldn't tell us either, but she was obviously desperate to confide in someone and there was an outside chance it was relevant. So when he mentioned she'd asked to talk to you, we thought . . .'

'That I could do your work for you,' Melissa interposed. 'Well, it so happens you were on the right track. Mrs Aggs *did* suspect her husband of being the Smiler, so take a Brownie point apiece.'

'But you said you put her mind at rest,' said Waters. 'What exactly did you tell her?'

'I asked her first of all if her husband had been out on a jolly during Saturday night, and she said definitely not. Then I told her how I'd found Martha Willis and how she'd been murdered some time during that night . . .'

'You didn't mention the smile, I hope,' Waters interrupted.

'Of course I didn't, what do you take me for?' she replied indignantly. 'What I said was, I understood the police were linking Martha's death with the Thanebury murders. I'm pretty sure she knows about the Smiler's nasty little trade mark, though.' She shuddered as she spoke; the memory still gave her gooseflesh.

'What makes you think so?' asked Waters.

'She asked . . . I can't remember the exact words . . . but she was anxious to know if there were any marks, no, if there was anything unusual about the body. Which is what the press are desperate to find out, by the way,' she added, remembering the reporters swarming on her doorstep earlier in the day.

'Tell us about it!' Waters rolled his eyes to the ceiling. 'Thank goodness we've managed to keep the identity of the girl who found the most recent victim a secret from them. It seems she rushed home in a state of hysteria, babbling about a dead woman with a smile. Her mother guessed something was seriously wrong and called a doctor, who put the girl under sedation and then informed the police. The poor kid's pretty traumatised; she still attends her college classes – she's an art student – but her mother says she's very withdrawn and hardly speaks to anyone. We're pretty sure some of the details are known in the village, but so far we've managed to keep them from the press. Thanebury people are a very close, tight-lipped bunch and they particularly dislike reporters.'

'I gathered that from a story in the *Gazette* a while back.'

'Yes, well, this latest murder has complicated things, I'm afraid.'

'In what way?'

'All the other victims lived in or around Thanebury. Everybody there knew them and they all knew one another. Thanebury is nearly twenty miles from Upper Benbury and so far we haven't traced anyone there connected with Martha. Why should the Smiler suddenly go so far afield for a victim?'

'I think I see what you're driving at.' Melissa's brain was ticking over fast and its conclusions were chilling. 'You're saying that if Mr Aggs' night-time excursions correspond to the dates of the first three murders, he could still be the original Smiler and . . .' The food she had just eaten seemed to be congealing in her stomach and she regarded her own helping of dessert with distaste.

'. . . and there's a copycat killer at work,' Waters finished quietly. 'Mind you, these are only initial thoughts.'

Harris paused with a spoonful of pie halfway to his mouth. 'By the way, Matt, the painted smile on Martha Willis's face – how closely did it match the others?'

'On an initial examination, very closely,' Waters replied. 'Of course, there'll be further tests, but allowing for the inevitable minor variations, they look remarkably similar.'

'So whoever killed Martha, if it wasn't the Smiler himself, must have seen at least one of the other victims. Not just seen them,' Harris went on, jabbing the air with his dessert spoon to emphasise his point, 'he must have had time to study them pretty carefully.'

'Agreed.'

'But you mentioned that a different colour lipstick was used this time?'

'Yes, but that in itself means nothing. The original one could have been used up, or lost, or the Smiler might just have fancied a change.'

'Did the doctor who attended the girl also see the body?'

'I understand she did, but she was on duty in the Casualty Department at Stowbridge Hospital the night Martha was killed.'

'So she's eliminated straight away.'

There was a brief silence while the pie was demolished. Then Harris pushed his plate away and leaned his elbows on the table. 'Let's recap,' he said. 'Who found the first body?'

'Our local man, PC Skinner. He noticed that Mrs Painter hadn't taken her milk in and went to investigate.'

'No sign of forced entry?'

'None – nor in any of the other cases. Whoever killed them must have used keys because the doors were still locked.' Waters ran his fingers through his thatch of greying hair in a gesture of exasperation. 'Thanebury people aren't exactly security conscious. Half of them don't bother to lock their doors at all during the day.'

'But this happened at night, so presumably the door was locked then. How did Skinner get in?'

'With the key the old lady used to hide under the doormat. That's another quaint local custom.'

Harris shook his head in despair at the folly of the elderly country dweller. 'Never learn, do they? Think they're still living in the nineteenth century. What about the next victim?'

'That was old Mr Eldridge. He'd been dead for at least a couple of days when he was found by the home help. Fortunately, she's a level-headed sort of woman and didn't panic, although she was naturally very shocked at what she saw.'

'And the third?'

'Miss Twigg. She was practically bedridden, although she could just manage to drag herself to the bathroom, make herself a cup of tea, that sort of thing. The social workers wanted her to go into a home, but she flatly refused. As it happens, there's a group of young people – members of the local church – who do a lot of voluntary work among the elderly. They used to take turns to pop in and see that she was all right, and she had meals on wheels and visits from the district nurse and so on.'

'Presumably the girl who found her was one of the volunteers?'

'Right.'

'And you're sure she hasn't told anyone about the smile?'

Waters shrugged. 'We think not, but of course, we can't be certain. As I said, she was so shocked by her discovery that she's hardly spoken to anyone since. At least, no one's leaked it to the press.'

'And the *modus operandi* was the same in every case?'

'Identical. Suffocation with the victim's own pillow, which was then replaced under the head.'

Melissa took advantage of a temporary break in the conversation to bring a cafetière, cups and saucers to the table. Both men looked up in surprise, as if they had forgotten her presence.

'Sorry, we shouldn't have spent all this time talking shop,' said Waters.

'No need to apologise,' she said, pouring coffee. 'Remember, murder is my bread and butter as well. Oh Lord!' She put a hand to her mouth. 'That sounds pretty callous, doesn't it – we're talking about real people here.'

'No good getting emotional about these things – it interferes with one's powers of reasoning,' observed

Harris, somewhat sententiously, as he spooned sugar into his coffee. 'You've been listening to our recap, Mel – any ideas?'

'Has anyone drawn up a profile of the killer?' she asked, after a moment's thought.

'We haven't asked for one by a professional shrink, but we've given it plenty of consideration, naturally,' said Waters. 'Des Holloway is trying to sell the Super a theory of his own to account for the smile.'

'Which is?'

'That we're looking for a local operator who kills for simple pleasure. He's too cunning to let that pleasure be seen on his own face, so he paints a smile on the faces of his victims. He also thinks the killer is probably a slightly-built man, or possibly a woman, since all the victims are frail and couldn't have put up much resistance.'

'In other words, the Smiler selects his victims on the basis of whether he – or she – feels strong enough to tackle them?'

'Have you an alternative suggestion?'

'I think so,' said Melissa slowly. 'Suppose the Smiler is some sort of religious crank who believes that death is simply the gateway to eternal bliss? He deludes himself into believing he's been entrusted with a sacred mission, which is to release from their earthly suffering lonely, housebound old people with – as he sees it – precious little to live for. He despatches them as painlessly as possible and sends them into the hereafter with a smile on their faces.'

There was a pause while the two men digested the hypothesis. 'It's pretty way-out . . . but feasible, I suppose,' muttered Harris. Waters looked dubious.

'What bothers me,' Melissa went on, half thinking

aloud, 'is why the Smiler should target Martha Willis. Apart from the question of distance, she doesn't fit in with the pattern of the Thanebury victims.'

'Why not?' said Waters. 'She was elderly, frail, living alone . . .'

'She wasn't by any means housebound and she still enjoyed life in her quiet way. She liked to be as independent as possible, she could walk short distances around the village and still took her turn on the church flower-arranging rota. And she pottered in her garden and lots of people used to call in to see her.'

'So the "happy release" motive doesn't apply to her?'

'I wouldn't have said so.'

'Which brings us back to the copycat theory.'

'I suppose,' said Harris thoughtfully, 'Aggs could still be our man.'

'But Mrs Aggs said he never went out that night,' Waters objected.

'Maybe he realised that she was getting suspicious. He could have put a sleeping pill in her cocoa, or whatever she drinks at bedtime.'

Waters sucked air through pursed lips as he considered the proposal. 'So that she'd never know he'd left the matrimonial bed? It's possible, I suppose, but it still doesn't explain why he came looking for a victim in Upper Benbury.' He shook his head doubtfully. 'Still, I think I'll suggest to the powers that be that we take a bit of interest in Mr Aggs.'

By mutual consent, the subject of the killings was dropped for the rest of the evening. When the two men finally began to take their leave, and while Waters was in the bathroom, Harris said, 'I'll come back after I've driven Matt home, if you like.'

'I'll be all right, really. I don't fit the profile of a Smiler victim. And besides,' she added as a new thought struck her. 'Even if the Smiler *is* going to strike again, it won't be for another couple of months.'

'What makes you say that?'

'Look at it this way. All four killings have been carried out at roughly two-monthly intervals, and Mrs Aggs left it for that length of time before making up her mind to come and see you. Supposing there had been other signs . . . Aggs getting fidgety or withdrawn, or otherwise acting strangely . . . she was on a knife-edge, reluctant to believe her husband capable of murder yet driven by her conscience to do something before it was too late.'

'In that case, and if Aggs is our man, her conscience didn't drive hard enough,' said Harris grimly. 'It'll be interesting to hear what CID manage to prise out of him. Meanwhile . . . ,' he reached for Melissa and held her close for a moment, then released her as they heard Waters returning. 'If you're sure you'll be all right on your own . . .'

'I'm sure. There's no earthly reason why he should pick on me.'

'You will check that all your doors and windows are locked?'

'I always do.'

'And, Mel . . . ?'

'What?'

'Don't get ideas about doing any sleuthing on your own, will you?'

'Such a thing never occurred to me,' she protested.

Which, at the time of speaking, was perfectly true.

Chapter Eight

When Melissa arrived at the rectory shortly after eleven o'clock on the Tuesday after the discovery of Martha Willis's body, there was an unfamiliar car, even older than the Hamleys' battered Cavalier, parked on the drive. She hesitated at the gate, thinking that she might have arrived at an inconvenient moment, might even have mistaken the time of the invitation. Then she spotted Alice at a downstairs window, waving and beckoning. By the time she reached the front door, it was open.

'I'm so glad you're here,' said Alice, a little breathlessly. 'John has a visitor who's anxious to meet you. They're in the study.' She led the way across the hall and indicated a half-open door from the other side of which came the sound of voices. 'Do go in,' she urged. 'I'll be with you in a minute – I'm just making some coffee.'

The two men who rose to greet Melissa presented an extraordinary contrast. John Hamley, with his short dark hair, clean-shaven face and neatly pressed suit worn over his clerical vest and collar, was the epitome of the conventional parson. The stranger had the appearance of an ageing hippie, with prominent brown eyes beneath a domed forehead and an untidy mass of greying hair that fell round his face and mingled with an equally luxuriant beard. His black cassock was shabby and, despite the chill of the March morning, he wore open sandals on sockless feet.

'May I introduce the Reverend Gareth Jarman, vicar of Saint Anne's Church in Thanebury?' said the rector. 'As I believe you know,' – he gave a nervous cough and jerked his head sideways towards his visitor – 'he and his parishioners have suffered, three times over, the same terrible tragedy that we have experienced here. He has very kindly come to offer us his sympathy and support. Mr Jarman, this is Mrs Craig, who had the unnerving experience of discovering poor Martha Willis's body.'

From the depths of the beard, a moist red mouth opened to reveal a double bank of glossy white teeth. Iron fingers encased Melissa's hand.

'I have a special message for you, dear Madam,' intoned the Reverend Jarman without giving her time to utter a word. 'You must not grieve for your late sister. Like those dear souls so recently departed from our parish, she has gone to eternal bliss. We who are left behind should give humble thanks for the life they led among us.' With the final pronouncement his voice, its Welsh lilt becoming stronger with every word, boomed to a crescendo and, releasing Melissa's hand, he raised both arms above his head like the popular conception of an Old Testament prophet.

'Er, yes, quite,' murmured Melissa, somewhat taken aback. She caught the rector's eye and realised that he was equally nonplussed by the patriarchal manner of his fellow cleric. It was a relief to both of them when Alice entered with the coffee.

'Milk and sugar, Mr Jarman?' she enquired.

'Thank you, no coffee for me.' He raised a large hand, like a policeman holding up traffic. 'I drink only water.

And please, call me Gareth,' he added, with a change of tone that made him sound almost normal.

'Oh, right. My name's Alice, and my husband is John, and . . . ,' she cast a doubtful glance at her second visitor, who nodded and said briskly, 'And I'm Melissa.'

'Melissa? Melissa Craig?' mused Gareth. 'A writer, I believe? I seem to have heard your name. Local history, is it?'

'Not exactly, although it is in a way local history that brings me here this morning.' Normally more than happy to respond to enquiries about her books, Melissa found herself reluctant to reveal their nature to the Reverend Gareth Jarman. She suspected that he might be moved to deliver a sermon on the evils of exploiting the baser appetites of the reading public. She turned to John Hamley. 'Alice mentioned that you wanted to ask me about Martha's background and her life in the village.'

'Yes, indeed, if you would be so kind.'

'And I told Melissa that if she felt counselling would help her get over her dreadful experience, she could come to you,' said Alice, obviously eager to promote her husband's skills.

'If Melissa would like professional counselling, she will need to find someone who doesn't know her personally,' he replied, giving her an affectionate pat on the shoulder. 'A counsellor should begin by being detached from the client. Of course,' he added, turning back to Melissa, 'if you feel that it would ease your mind to talk about it, I'm always ready, as a friend, to give an ear.'

'Absolutely! Ab-so-lutely!' boomed Gareth, so loudly that everyone jumped and Alice almost dropped her coffee cup. 'Exactly what I told my little group of handmaidens, my Daughters of Light. Talk to me, my children!' I said to them. 'Unburden your souls of their distress, empty your minds of all thoughts of vengeance and fill them with thankfulness for the Lord's mercy!'

John cleared his throat and said, 'Naturally, one can only agree with what you say about the Lord's mercy, but you surely aren't suggesting that murderers should go unpunished?'

The Reverend Gareth Jarman's sombre eyes seemed to glow with an inner fire. With flaring nostrils and upraised hand, he enjoined his hearers to remember the words of Saint Paul to the Romans. '"Vengeance *is* mine; I will repay, saith the Lord."' he intoned. In the stunned silence that followed, he rose majestically to his feet, drained with a flourish the glass of water that Alice had brought him and strode to the door, his cassock billowing around his naked ankles. 'I leave you now to visit a sick parishioner. Good day to you all, and God bless you!' With that, he swept from the room. Mumbling something about seeing him out, the rector hurried after him.

Left on their own, Alice and Melissa sat back in their chairs and exchanged bemused glances. Then they collapsed into giggles.

'Can you imagine what his sermons must be like?' gasped Alice, putting a handkerchief over her mouth to stifle her laughter.

'Full of saints marching in and Glory Glory Alleluiah, I expect,' chuckled Melissa. 'He put me in mind of the old revivalist preachers at open-air prayer meetings. I can just picture him on a windswept Welsh mountainside, haranguing the multitude like a latter-day John Wesley.'

'Still,' said Alice, when she had her voice under control, 'I suppose it's better at times like this to take a more, well, positive line. I mean, we must have faith that these poor people have gone to a better place. Don't you agree, John?' she appealed to her husband, who re-entered at that moment.

'Naturally, one must believe that,' he said solemnly, helping himself to more coffee. Then he, too, appeared struck by the humour of the situation. 'Can you imagine Major and Mrs Ford's reaction if I went round the parish looking like that?'

'Or if you expressed similar views on punishment,' Melissa said wryly.

'He's certainly eccentric, but I believe his flock think very highly of him, especially the young people. He holds special services for them on Sunday evenings and I'm told the church is always packed.'

'What the Fords would call "happy-clappy", I suppose,' remarked Alice.

'I imagine his "handmaidens", his "Daughters of Light" as he calls them, are the group of young volunteers who've been doing community service among the elderly in the parish,' said Melissa thoughtfully. 'It was one of them who found the third victim there,' she explained in response to enquiring looks from Alice and John. 'The poor girl was badly shaken, so I'm told.' Just in time, she remembered not to mention the smile.

Alice gave a little shiver. 'Understandably,' she said. 'I'll leave you two now to have your talk about Martha, if that's all right.' She loaded the coffee cups onto a tray and withdrew.

'I'm not sure I can be of much help,' said Melissa as the rector settled at his desk and opened a notebook, 'but I can give you the names of a few people that Martha used to associate with before her heart attack. For example, the members of a flower club in Cheltenham – as you know, she was very good at flower arranging – and I believe she used to do part-time work in a local nursery. She was a keen gardener and knew a lot about plants . . .'

For fifteen minutes or so, she sifted her memory for useful scraps of information while the rector made notes. At last she said, 'I think that's all I can tell you, but if anything else occurs to me I'll let you know.'

'You're very kind. That's been a great help,' he said warmly. 'I hope I haven't taken up too much of your time.'

'Not at all.'

He put away the notebook and got to his feet. 'Please excuse me if I rush away now. I have to meet the churchwarden to discuss repairs to some pews.'

'Of course, no problem.'

'I'll ask Alice to see you out. And please remember,' he added from the doorway, 'if ever you feel the need to talk about, you know . . .'

'I know. Thank you.'

As Melissa left the study, Alice appeared from the kitchen. 'I wonder if, before you go, I could ask you another favour?' she said.

'What is it?'

'Do you know Mrs Grantley-Newcombe?'

'Never heard of her. Does she live locally?'

'In Carston – one of the other parishes in John's rectorship. She bought the Manor House last year and she's spent a fortune renovating it – they say she's loaded with money. She phoned while you and John were talking.'

'And?'

'She's in a bit of a flap. She's just taken over as president of the Friends of Stowbridge Hospital and at her first committee meeting, which she called to discuss the fund-raising programme, the organising secretary announced her resignation.'

Melissa eyed Alice with dawning suspicion. 'You aren't suggesting that I take on the job?' she said warily.

Alice made little fluttering movements with her hands. 'Oh no, not at all, that is, not on a regular basis, just, well, their annual Nearly New sale is on next month and she's desperate. She thinks she's got someone who'll fill the vacancy after Easter, but this person can't do it before then because her daughter's having a baby and, well, Mrs Grantley-Newcombe is a very generous supporter of the church and I'd like to help her out if I can . . . and besides, wouldn't it sort of help to take your mind off, you know . . .' Alice paused, whether from shortage of breath or because she had run out of arguments was unclear.

'Of course, I know how much time you spend on your writing,' she hurried on after a moment, 'but you did mention you'd just finished a book and I thought perhaps you wouldn't mind, just this once . . .' The expression on her small, almost childlike face reminded Melissa of a puppy pleading for a biscuit.

'What sort of woman is this Mrs – what did you say her name was?'

'Mrs Grantley-Newcombe. She's, well, it's rather difficult to describe her without sounding snobbish. She's from London, very beautiful and charming, but I've heard one or two people describe her as ostentatious and *nouveau riche*. She does have a rather phoney posh accent, if you know what I mean. And she's also inclined to be bossy. Between you and me,' Alice dropped her voice, although no one was within earshot, 'I shouldn't be surprised if that's why Mrs Delaney resigned. The previous president was a very easy-going lady who let Mrs D have things more or less her own way.'

'And Mrs Grantley-Newcombe is wielding the proverbial new broom,' said Melissa with a smile. 'That does tend to upset the old guard, especially if the new broom is a comparative stranger. Well, it's in a good cause . . . and as long as it's clearly understood it's just for this one event . . .'

'Oh, bless you, Melissa. Is it all right if I give Mrs Grantley-Newcombe your phone number?'

'Why not? Look, I'd better be going now. Thank you for the coffee.'

'Thank you for all your help.' Her face alight with gratitude, Alice escorted Melissa to the door and stood there waving as she walked to the gate.

The weather, which had been dull and misty first thing, had cleared; birds twittered and darted to and fro, the sunlight glistened on wet grass and the rain-washed road leading through the village reflected the blue of the sky. Her spirits somewhat lightened, Melissa set off for home.

On the way, she thought back with some amusement to the encounter with the Reverend Gareth Jarman. What a bizarre character – she would surely be able to use him in some future novel. As she recalled the cadence of his voice and his choice of language, one phrase came repeatedly to mind. He had spoken of eternal bliss. Someone else had said the same thing, quite recently. Who was it?

She was almost home before she remembered. She herself had used the words the previous evening when she, Matt Waters and Ken Harris had been speculating on the motive that drove the Smiler to kill.

Chapter Nine

The next day was Wednesday. Punctually at nine o'clock, Gloria Parkin, the bouncy, blonde mother of three who 'did' for Melissa and – when she was in residence – her next-door neighbour Iris, arrived at Hawthorn Cottage to carry out her weekly three-hour stint of cleaning and polishing, at the same time bringing the latest gossip from around the combined parishes of Upper and Lower Benbury. On this particular morning, the shocking events of Sunday were uppermost in her mind.

'Just dreadful about Miss Willis, innit!' she exclaimed the moment she came through the door. 'Poor old lady! I never used to do for her 'cos she had a home help from the Council, but she were in church doing the flowers sometimes when I were there to do the brasses. Such a sweet old thing. And it were you what found her, is that right?' She gazed at Melissa with a mixture of awe and excitement in her toffee-brown eyes. 'Were there lots of blood?'

'None at all, she'd been suffocated. It said so in the papers – didn't you read the reports?'

'Oh, they newspapers never gets it right,' Gloria asserted cheerfully. 'They spelt my Stanley's name wrong once, and the name of his company as well – ever so cross, he were, went to the office to complain about it.'

Melissa suppressed a smile at the high-sounding description of Stanley Parkin's second-hand car business, located on a patch of open ground in Gloucester. 'How did his name come to be in the paper?' she asked. 'I don't remember reading about it.'

'Oh, it were ages ago. The coppers tried to make out he'd been fiddling the mileage on a car what he sold, but he never. He told the beak it were right as far as he knew, he bought the car in good faith and if it were fiddled it weren't him.'

'And did the magistrate believe him?'

'Course he did!' Gloria's plump features expressed outrage at the thought of anyone doubting her husband's word. 'My Stanley's never been caught fiddling nothing!' she declared virtuously.

Melissa forebore to mention that not being caught was not quite the same thing as being innocent. As far as Gloria was concerned Stanley Parkin, generous provider for herself and their bonny children, could do no wrong.

'Tell you what, though,' said Gloria, reverting to the original topic while tying on her apron and rolling up the sleeves of her brightly patterned blouse, 'one of my ladies in Lower Benbury, her daughter's in the office at the art college, and she told her Mum, and her Mum told me yesterday, one of the teachers told her it were one of the students there what found the last old lady what got done in at Thanebury.'

'Really?' said Melissa, after a moment spent mentally unravelling this complex statement. 'What else did she say?'

'Nothing much, 'cept the girl still hardly speaks to no one, just sits in the corner of the classroom drawing pictures.'

'She must have been badly shocked. Finding a dead person is very upsetting,' Melissa pointed out.

'Ooh my, yes, of course. Was you very shocked when you found Miss Willis?'

'A bit, but I'm all right now.'

'That's good. Well, I'd better get on. Start with the bathroom, shall I?' Since this was her normal routine, Gloria picked up her bucket of cleaning materials and set off upstairs without waiting for a reply.

The morning post included a card from Iris with a view of a sun-drenched lavender field in the South of France. The message was typically laconic: 'Home Friday. Please buy milk and bread and tell Gloria. Love to you and Binkie, Iris.' Immediately, Melissa's spirits lifted. It would be good to have her friend back again. Although the two women lived separate lives in their adjacent cottages, each busy with her own career, they enjoyed an undemanding companionship that went far deeper than mere neighbourliness. Melissa glanced across the kitchen to where Iris's cherished half-Persian cat snoozed happily by the Aga and said, 'Binkie, your Mum'll be home soon, isn't that good news?' Binkie opened one eye and responded with a brief, full-throated purr before dozing off again.

At eleven o'clock, Melissa prepared coffee, which she and Gloria drank together in the kitchen. Having passed on Iris's message, she remembered her conversation with Alice Hamley the previous day and asked, 'Do you happen to know a Mrs Grantley-Newcombe?'

Gloria tilted her head on one side and helped herself to a second ginger biscuit while considering. 'I've heard of her, can't think where,' she said. 'She don't live in Benbury.'

'No, I believe she lives in Carston Manor.'

'Oh, her!' Gloria crunched the biscuit between her small white teeth, flicked crumbs from her blouse and took a swig of coffee. 'My Stanley's Auntie Muriel knows her,' she announced with some pride. 'Well, not knows her, exactly, knows about her, so to speak.'

In the course of researching a novel, Melissa had once paid a visit to Stanley Parkin's aunt, who had spent many years as a lady's maid in some of the 'best' families in London and still maintained a lively interest in the doings of the leisured classes. If Mrs Grantley-Newcombe fell into this category, Miss Muriel Parkin would certainly know all that was worth knowing.

'It were when Mrs G-N's picture were in the paper a while back,' explained Gloria, who needed no encouragement to air her knowledge. 'Something to do with Stowbridge Hospital, it were.'

'She's just taken over as president of the Friends of the Hospital.'

'Thassit. Got a bit of a shady past, according to Auntie Muriel.' Gloria gave a meaning wink. 'Seems she was some rich bloke's bit on the side and he left her all his money. His ex were furious!' Gloria's exuberant mirth set her ample breasts shaking beneath the floral blouse.

'Fancy that,' said Melissa, thinking that her new commitment might turn out to be more interesting than she had anticipated. 'How long ago did all this happen? I mean, when did she inherit the money?'

'Dunno exactly. She had to wait a while before she got her hands on it 'cos the ex tried to put a stop to it.'

'You mean, she contested the will?'

'Thassright. Spent a fortune on lawyers and things, and then lost!' For some reason, this too appealed to Gloria's sense of humour. 'A right old hatchet-face, the ex were, but Mrs G–N's a real glamourpuss. They both had their pictures in *Today*. The ex had a face like a wet weekend, but Mrs G-N looked ever so pleased with herself!' The recollection set Gloria's bosom jiggling afresh. 'Course, she called herself something else then.'

'But you don't remember how long ago this was?'

'Sorry.'

One could always find out – although, Melissa reminded herself, there was no particular reason to do so. *I've spent too long writing fiction*, she thought, *this is becoming an obsession. I'm seeing everyone I meet as a potential character for a novel.* She got up from the table and carried the empty coffee mugs to the sink. Gloria took the hint and slid from her chair.

'Better get back to work,' she said.

Friday was mild and bright, with a blue sky behind a thin layer of broken cloud that resembled a veil of tattered lace. Iris arrived home during the afternoon; her veteran Morris came bumping along the track just as Melissa was returning from a brisk walk along the valley. The two friends hugged one another while Binkie, who had been dozing on a wall in the sunshine, performed figures of eight round his mistress's legs, purring like a pneumatic drill. Iris caught him up in her arms and crooned, 'Aah! Did my Binkie-Winkie miss his Muvver then?' with her cheek buried in his fur and an imbecilic grin on her face.

'Iris, you look wonderful!' said Melissa warmly, too delighted at her friend's return to feel her normal irritation at the baby-talk. She studied the tanned features and lean figure with envy. 'How come you never put on an ounce, no matter how much you eat?'

'Healthy diet.' Iris was a committed vegetarian. 'Told you hundreds of times.'

They had had this discussion on a number of occasions and got nowhere. To change the subject, Melissa said, 'Shall I give you a hand with your luggage?'

'Thanks.' Iris put the cat down and turned her attention to unloading her assortment of battered holdalls and artist's impedimenta. When everything had been carried into Elder Cottage and Iris, after a brief tour of inspection, was satisfied that all was as it should be, the two repaired to the kitchen of Hawthorn Cottage to drink tea and exchange news.

Iris, never loquacious, had even less than usual to say about her stay in the small French village south of Avignon where she regularly spent the winter. She brushed aside Melissa's questions and demanded to be brought up to date with events in Upper Benbury.

'Things have been pretty grim here these past few days,' Melissa said. The hideous memory came back with a rush as she told of finding Martha Willis's body; before she could stop herself, she blurted out every detail and then sat with her hands over her eyes, reliving the moment of discovery. Despite her earlier assertions, she was still badly affected by the experience.

Iris came over and put an arm round her shoulders. 'Should have phoned and told me. I'd have come right away. Not good to be on your own.'

'I haven't been on my own the whole time. Ken stayed on Sunday night and he and Matt Waters were here for supper on Monday. I'd more or less got over it by then, or at least, I thought I had. I mean, I'm not scared to be in the place alone . . . it's just . . . I can't get that awful painted smile out of my head. Iris, promise me you won't breathe a word about that to anyone. The police are worried some copycat weirdo might hear about it.'

'Course I won't.' Iris returned to her chair. 'So what've the fuzz turned up?'

'Nothing new, so far as I know. Ken's been in Birmingham on a surveillance job since Wednesday, so he won't have spoken to any of his old mates at the nick.'

'Do they believe it was the Thanebury killer who did for Martha?'

'I don't know – I imagine they're keeping an open mind.'

'What about you?'

'I'm not sure what to believe, but the more I think about it, the more doubtful it seems. But if it wasn't, that leaves several baffling questions.'

'Hmm.' Iris refilled her cup with hot water and dunked a herbal teabag in it. 'Any other news?'

'Nothing special that I haven't told you in my letters. Alice Hamley has recruited me to help at some up-market charity jumble sale and the Donovans are anxious for you to pay them a call. They were at the Fords' party; it was the first time old Cluny Donovan had come out of hiding, but he's not really with it. He hasn't got over his son's death.'

'Heard at the time he'd taken it badly,' said Iris.

'When did it happen?'

'Quite a while ago – can't remember exactly. OD'd on drugs and alcohol, so I heard. Awful tragedy.'

'It's had a shattering effect on the family. The girls persuaded their father to move out of London, thinking a change of environment would help, but he hasn't responded – he's still like a zombie. The mother has gone back to her family in Poland and as for Sirry and Genty . . . well, I think they live from day to day, hoping things will improve.'

'Poor things.' Iris absently turned her teacup between her hands. 'I met Saxe once. Good-looking lad. Promising artist, people said.' She drained the cup and put it down. 'I'll pay them a call when I've settled in.'

'They'll be delighted to see you. I think they're hoping that contact with a fellow artist might help Cluny snap out of it.'

'I'll do what I can.'

'They were very upset by Martha's death. They've been so kind to her. They don't want the old man to know it was murder, by the way.'

'I'll remember.' Iris stood up, flexing her arms and shoulders. 'Must go and unwind, then unpack. Thanks for the tea.'

'Why not come for supper?' Melissa suggested. 'Aubergine and tomato flan,' she added, anticipating the inevitable question. 'It's a new recipe – I think you'll like it.'

'Sounds good. Thanks.'

Chapter Ten

In church on Sunday morning, the rector read aloud a message of sympathy from the Reverend Gareth Jarman. He also announced that a memorial service for all victims of the recent dreadful wave of killings was being held that evening in the village church in Thanebury. Martha Willis would be remembered in the prayers and her friends were welcome to attend.

'You going?' asked Iris as she and Melissa walked home.

'Yes, I think so. It might help to lay Martha's ghost. We don't know yet when the police will release her body for burial. Will you come with me?'

'Of course. By the way, what time are we expected at the Donovans?' A pressing invitation to both of them for Sunday tea had been issued during the week.

'Three o'clock.'

'Right. See you about five to.'

When they arrived at Larkfield Barn they were greeted with warm smiles by Sirry and Genty and ushered into the sitting-room, where they found Cluny seated in an armchair in front of the fire, his gaze fixed on the portrait over the mantelpiece.

'Father, here's someone to see you – one of your former students,' said Sirry in the brisk, artificially bright voice of someone visiting a chronic invalid. 'She remembers you very well.'

Cluny gave no sign of being aware of their presence and neither moved nor spoke. The sisters exchanged glances; Genty moved towards her father with a hand outstretched as if intending to give him a shake, but Iris intervened by stepping forward and standing beside his chair. With her hands loosely clasped behind her, she looked up at the portrait and said, in her most matter-of-fact voice, 'Saxe Donovan. Good likeness. Your work?'

For a moment, there was no response. Then, without taking his gaze from the portrait, Cluny said quietly, 'You knew my son?'

'Met him once at an exhibition. Good-looking chap. Talented too. Must have been a blow, losing him.' Without waiting for a reply, Iris swung round to face Cluny and held out a hand. 'Iris Ash. Ravenswood. Nineteen sixty two to four.'

'Ravenswood?' he repeated. He did not look round, but his voice held a flicker of interest. 'The College of Art and Design?'

'Right.'

'What was the name again?'

'Iris Ash.'

This time he turned his head to look at her. Slowly he stood up, took the outstretched hand and peered into her face. 'The name sounds familiar.'

'Used to attend your life class,' said Iris. 'Never much good at bodies, I'm afraid.'

'I remember!' Cluny's demeanour underwent a gradual but dramatic change. Like a puppet coming to life after being struck by a magician's wand, he slowly drew himself up to his full height. Recognition dawned in his eyes.

'Not much good?' he repeated. 'Ha! You were bloody useless! I never had a student with less idea of how the human form is constructed.' He released her hand and pointed to a chair. 'Sit down!' he commanded.

'Thanks. Prefer the floor.' Without ceremony, Iris plumped herself down on the hearthrug and tucked her feet under her full skirt. Wearing a humble expression that only someone who knew her as well as Melissa would have recognised as assumed, she looked up at her old tutor and said, 'Was I really that bad?'

'You were hopeless, so you were!' he declared after resuming his own seat. 'You managed to make the best-looking model we ever had look like a deformed leprechaun. What was her name now? Daphne, Dolly . . . ?'

Iris shrugged and shook her head. 'Forget the name. Remember the girl. Skinny little thing.'

'Skinny!' he roared. 'That just shows how little you know about proportion. A Venus in miniature, that was Dolly . . . or whatever her name was.' He waved a dismissive hand, implying that a name that could not be recalled was of no importance.

'If you say so,' said Iris, the sparkle in her grey eyes belying the meekness in her tone. It occurred to Melissa that with her sharp features and lean frame she was not unlike a leprechaun herself, seated cross-legged in the firelight.

'You know your trouble?' Cluny leaned forward and waggled an accusing forefinger a few inches from her nose. 'You gave up too easily. You didn't practise enough. What did I always tell you, what did I tell all me students? Practice makes perfect, that's what I always told them.' His Irish accent became more pronounced as he mounted his favourite hobby-horse. 'That's what

I tell all me students and that's what I tell me darlin' girls, do I not?' He swung round towards the sofa where Sirry and Genty sat with Melissa, all three marvelling at the change in him.

'Yes, you do, Father. Practice makes perfect!' chanted his daughters. As at the Fords' party, they exchanged knowing smiles; this was obviously a family joke of long standing.

Cluny turned back to Iris. 'So what have you done with yourself since Ravenswood?' he demanded.

'Fabric and wallpaper design mostly. A few water-colours of country houses and gardens. No call for bodies there,' replied Iris cheerfully.

Cluny looked down at her with a hint of disdain on his well-cut features. 'Chocolate boxes and Christmas cards!' he scoffed. 'You'll never make a name for yourself with that sort of rubbish.'

'Might be rubbish, but doesn't do too badly. Pays the bills.' It was evidently no part of Iris's plan to boast about her own work, which had earned international recognition. She merely sat with her hands folded in her lap and a peaceful smile on her face, waiting for Cluny to lead the discussion in whatever direction he chose.

Melissa detected a movement at her side and saw Genty indicating to Sirry that they should retire. She followed them as they slipped quietly out of the room and went into the kitchen, where a tray laden with tea-things stood ready on the table.

Genty filled the kettle and plugged it in. 'We thought we'd leave them on their own while we make the tea,' she said.

'Good idea,' agreed Melissa. 'Iris seems to have hit the right note straight away.'

'It's wonderful to see him so animated,' said Sirry. 'I don't remember the last time he showed a positive interest in anything. Perhaps this is the breakthrough we've been praying for.'

'I do hope so, for all your sakes.'

Their optimism was short-lived. When they returned to the sitting-room with the tea-tray, Cluny had resumed his original attitude, his gaze fixed on the portrait. Iris, who was still sitting on the hearthrug, got to her feet as they entered and came towards them, ruefully shaking her head.

'Afraid he's gone off the boil,' she said in a low voice. 'My fault, trying to rush things. Asked what he's working on now, and he just . . . went. Wrong thing to say, I suppose.'

'Don't blame yourself,' said Sirry. 'You made real headway for a while – we haven't seen him like that since Saxe died.' Her voice wavered and her lips trembled; she put the tray on the table and spent several seconds stirring the contents of the teapot, her head bent forward to hide her emotion. Genty went to her side and took her free hand in both her own, gripping it and giving it a slight shake. Their eyes met; they exchanged the briefest of nods before Sirry raised her head again and asked, with a forced smile, whether the guests would prefer milk or lemon in their tea. Melissa had the impression that some unspoken message had passed between the sisters, some inner strength transmitted from the younger to the elder.

Conversation for the remainder of the visit was desultory. Iris did her best to reanimate Cluny's interest with odd items of news of past students at Ravenswood, but although he responded politely and even smiled once or twice, he made no contribution of his own. It was a relief when it was timc to go.

At the front door, Genty said, 'Are you going to the service in Thanebury.'

'We thought we would,' said Melissa. 'What about you?'

'Yes, I'm going. We – Sirry and I – felt one of us should. We owe it to Martha. Besides, it was one of my students who found Miss Twigg's body and she asked me to be there. Poor thing, she's still dreadfully upset.'

'Yes, so I heard. My help knows someone who works at the college,' she added in response to Genty's look of surprise. 'Would you like to come with us?'

'I'd rather use my own car, thanks all the same. We don't want Father asking questions – he doesn't know how Martha died, you see, so it would be tricky explaining. We've told him I'm going to meet one of my students who's been having some problems.'

'Fair enough.'

'I'll give you a lift if you like.' She glanced from one to the other, and they smiled and nodded acceptance. 'Shall I pick you up about six o'clock?'

'Thanks. See you then. And thank you for the tea.'

'Thank you for coming. I do hope you'll come again.' This time, Genty spoke directly to Iris. 'Bring some of your work to show him,' she suggested.

Iris grinned. 'Not a bad idea. Let him tear it to shreds, then show me how it should be done.'

'Those girls bear a heavy burden,' Melissa remarked as they walked home down the lane. 'It was good of them to find time to befriend Martha.'

'Shows a nice spirit,' Iris agreed.

* * *

It is believed that there was a church in Upper Benbury in Saxon times, although the present building dates back no earlier than the eleventh century, when it was recorded in the *Domesday Book*. It is noted for its Norman tower and chancel arch, its beamed roof, the stained glass in its Early English windows, its carved stone pulpit and ornate brass lectern. It boasts a number of historic memorials and relics, and a celebrated peal of bells which from time to time draws enthusiastic teams of visiting ringers.

In contrast, the parish church in Thanebury was built less than ten years after the Second World War and reflects in its construction and furnishings the austerity of the period. It is a squat, rectangular structure with a slate roof and a small tower shaped like an old-fashioned dovecote, from which a single bell calls the congregation to worship. The interior is equally unpretentious; the pulpit and lectern are of wood and, like the pews, have little or no decoration. On the altar are a plain brass cross and candlesticks; there are few pictures and only clear glass in the windows.

Yet it was evident to Melissa, sitting between Iris and Genty as they waited for the service to begin, that this was a building no less loved and cared for than many an ancient place of worship. Everything was spotless; the warm air held a hint of pine-scented polish and the woodwork gleamed in the light shed by simple modern fittings. Concealed behind a pillar, an organist played soft music and there were fresh flowers everywhere, beautifully arranged.

And the church was packed to overflowing. It seemed as if the entire population of the tiny village had squeezed itself inside and now waited quietly for the service to begin. A number of those present were middle-aged to elderly, but so far as Melissa could see, Mrs Aggs was not among them.

There was also a fair sprinkling of young people. Across the aisle, in the pew opposite the one where she and the others were sitting, Melissa noticed a group of girls whom she judged to be in their late teens or early twenties. They looked like students; they had pale, solemn faces, wore no make-up and were almost identically dressed in dark clothes with striped woollen scarves round their necks. She put her lips to Iris's ear and whispered, 'I wonder if they're the Reverend Jarman's Daughters of Light?'

Iris, who had earlier chuckled over Melissa's account of her meeting with the eccentric cleric, followed her glance. 'Could be,' she whispered back. 'The one this end looks a bit twitchy.'

'Perhaps she's the one Genty was telling us about.'

At that moment, the girl in question turned and looked in their direction. Genty said, 'Can we all move up a little so that Natalie can sit with me?'

'Of course.' Melissa and Iris shuffled sideways and Genty beckoned to the girl, who nodded eagerly and started to rise, but was held back by her neighbour. There seemed to be an urgent consultation among the members of the group, after which, with a shrug of the shoulders and a look of resignation, Natalie settled back into her seat. At that moment, the music died and the Reverend Gareth Jarman made his entrance.

He strode up the aisle and turned to face his congregation. In a few well-chosen words he explained the purpose and order of the service. Some prayers were said and four hymns sung, each followed by a short reading dedicated to one of the departed and given by a different member of the congregation. The passage chosen for Martha Willis was read by the Rector of Benbury, the Reverend John Hamley.

The Reverend Jarman then invited everyone to pray quietly for a short period. Most people knelt, except for a few of the more elderly who sat with heads bowed. The silence that settled over the congregation had an almost unearthly quality. No one coughed or fidgeted and it seemed as if everyone was holding their breath. There was something hypnotic about it; Melissa felt as if she was falling into a trance when, without warning, a voice boomed out from above her head.

'In the Name of the Father, and of the Son . . .'

She opened her eyes. The Reverend Jarman had climbed noiselessly into the pulpit and was making the sign of the cross with his right hand. Heads were lifted, those who were kneeling resumed their seats and everyone settled down to listen. Someone had dimmed the lights, except for a single bulb which shone directly down on the man in the pulpit. He made a striking figure, standing erect with his head tilted slightly backwards, his hands resting on the wooden rail as he gazed down at the faces raised to his. After a pause that verged on the theatrical, he delivered the words of his text: *Be thou faithful unto death and I will give thee a crown of life.*

'We are not here to grieve for our lately departed sisters and brother,' he began, 'nor yet to dwell on the nature of their departure, but to give humble and hearty thanks for the joy that is now theirs. For they have entered into eternal bliss.'

Those words again. Melissa suppressed a shudder; they had the effect of reviving the sick horror she had felt when standing alone in Martha Willis's bedroom, exactly a week ago. Determinedly, she pushed the memory to one side and tried to concentrate on the preacher's words, but found her attention as much held by his physical presence as by what he was saying. His eyes glittered, his abundant hair shone silver in the lamplight, his large hands made sweeping gestures or gripped the edge of the pulpit as he leaned forward to make some telling point. His lilting Welsh voice, now loud and resonant, now falling to a thrilling whisper, seemed to re-echo from every corner as, drawing heavily on the Book of Revelation but using many powerful images of his own, he spoke of the new heaven and the new earth, of gates and angels, of buildings of gold and jasper and glass. By any standards, he was a gifted orator, speaking without notes and without hesitation. His mouth, moving within the thick mass of beard and taking on a new shape with each individual word, seemed like some protean creature that had developed a life of its own. The peroration rolled on, but Melissa was no longer listening. She could think of nothing, see nothing but those moist, red lips.

It reminds me of Martha when I found her. I can't bear much more of this. I shouldn't have come. She was mesmerised, like a rabbit caught in headlights, unable to drag her gaze from the figure in the pulpit. Then she felt someone shaking her by the arm and, with an effort, turned her head to see Iris peering at her.

'You all right?'

The voice was still thundering around them, but the nightmare vision faded as she met her friend's look of concern. She drew a deep breath and whispered, 'Yes, but I'm finding this hard to take.'

'You're not the only one.' Iris jerked her head sideways and Melissa followed her glance to where the girls were sitting. Three were gazing up at the preacher with expressions of adoration on their young faces; the fourth, Natalie, sat rigid, her eyes glazed. She, too, was reliving a personal nightmare.

Mercifully, a few minutes later and with surprising abruptness, the service was brought to a close and the blessing given. A subdued congregation filed into the porch, where the Reverend Jarman was waiting to greet each worshipper with outstretched hand and radiant smile. There was no way that Melissa could avoid the contact, but it was all she could do to repress a shudder as his fingers closed over hers.

Outside, Genty attempted to approach Natalie, who showed every sign of wanting to talk to her but was hustled unceremoniously away by her friends.

'I don't understand why they won't let her talk to me,' said Genty, looking troubled.

'Perhaps they're afraid she'll break down, have hysterics or something,' suggested Melissa.

They watched the little group retreating, then Genty turned away with a shrug. 'Oh well, that's that, I suppose. May as well go back to the car.'

'Rum bunch that,' commented Iris as they waited for Genty to unlock the doors. 'The way those girls sat there looking gobsmacked, as if they were hearing a new Messiah. Unhealthy, if you ask me.'

Even as Iris was speaking, a chilling thought had crept into Melissa's mind. 'Not just unhealthy. Dangerous,' she said.

Chapter Eleven

Very little was said during the journey back to Upper Benbury. The weather had turned wet with a blustery wind and Genty needed all her concentration for driving. Iris, seated beside her, was her normal taciturn self while Melissa, huddled into the back seat and staring blankly out of the streaming windows, was deep in her own thoughts.

When they were nearly home, Iris said to Genty, 'No need to go right to the door. Drop us in the lane.'

'Are you sure? It's still raining.'

'Not much now. Turning's tricky in the dark. That okay with you, Mel?'

'What?' The sound of her name brought Melissa out of her reverie. 'Oh, yes, of course,' she agreed as Iris repeated her suggestion. 'It's only a few yards to our front doors and I've got a torch in my handbag.'

'Well, if you're sure.' Genty pulled in and stopped, leaving the engine running. Melissa and Iris scrambled out, repeated their thanks and said good night. The damp wind tugged at their clothes as they picked their way through the puddles in the uneven track.

'Had any supper?' asked Iris, fishing out her latch-key.

'Only a sandwich and a cup of tea before we left.'

'Can't last till breakfast on that. Come and share my veggie stroganoff.'

'I'd like that – thanks.'

'You can tell me about it while I'm warming it up.'

'About what?'

'Whatever was bugging you on the way home.'

'What makes you think . . . ?'

'Saw your face when you were shaking hands with the hot-gospeller. Don't like him, do you?'

During this exchange, they had shed their outdoor things and made their way into the kitchen, where Iris began bustling about, setting a pan on the Aga to reheat and taking plates and cutlery from cupboards and drawers. Melissa sat down at the table and leaned wearily back in her chair.

'I've no reason to dislike him,' she said slowly, 'but there's something about him that disturbs me. It's . . . oh, I can't put my finger on it, but . . .' She broke off; there was no rational explanation for her unease and she could not bring herself to admit to Iris the parallel that her over-charged imagination had drawn between the loquacious lips of the Reverend Jarman and the disgusting disfigurement that the Smiler inflicted on the dead faces of his victims. It was an illogical fantasy, a total irrelevance that made no sense whatever. Iris would, quite rightly, scold her for letting her fancy run away with her, for allowing herself to be affected like an emotional schoolgirl by the Reverend Jarman's 'hot-gospelling'.

'Think I know what you mean,' Iris was saying. 'Too much glorification of the hereafter for impressionable young minds. Could give them a morbid interest in death.' Her expression was thoughtful as she stirred the contents of the pan. 'Not healthy,' she asserted for the second time that evening.

'You're speaking of those girls in the pew opposite ours?' said Melissa. 'I think Genty was hurt at not being able to talk to Natalie. She seems to feel protective towards her.'

'One of her students,' Iris reminded her. 'Only natural. Was your Mrs Aggs in church, by the way?'

'I didn't see her. I wouldn't have spoken to her anyway. If her husband was there as well, she'd have been embarrassed.'

'How so?'

'Didn't I tell you? She was terrified of being spotted with me, in case she had to explain it to someone.'

'Funny woman. Understandable though. Disreputable lot, crime writers.' Through the steam from the pan, grey eyes twinkled in mockery.

'Almost as bad as artists,' Melissa agreed. She felt herself beginning to unwind.

'Here, tuck into that.' Iris put two plates of food on the table and poured out glasses of mineral water.

Melissa gave a rapturous sniff. 'Iris, this smells divine!'

'Hope it tastes as good. Help yourself to bread.'

When they had taken the edge off their appetites, Iris asked, 'How did your PC Plod get on in Birmingham?'

Melissa pulled a face at her. 'Do you have to call him that? Anyway, you know perfectly well Ken's left the Force.'

'Sorry.' Iris gave an unrepentant grin. 'PI Plod then.'

'You only call him that to annoy me.' Melissa pretended to take offence, but the grin merely broadened and she found herself smiling back as the banter made its own contribution to the easing in tension. 'He phoned on Friday to say another job had come up so he's staying over till tomorrow,' she said. 'He might have called this evening and left a message – I'll find out when I get home.'

'Surprised you didn't rush in to check straight away, the way things have been going,' Iris teased.

'Actually, I'm trying to play it cool. He seems to think that letting him stay the other night was a turning-point in our relationship.'

Iris cocked an eyebrow. 'Downhill all the way from now on?'

'That's his idea.'

'But not yours?'

Melissa disposed of her last mouthful of vegetable stroganoff and laid down her fork. 'I don't know,' she sighed. 'I do care for him, quite a lot, but I'm not sure I'm ready for a total commitment. Besides, Hawthorn Cottage isn't big enough for two.'

'And you don't want to leave?'

'Not just yet. Why this inquisition?'

'No reason. Just curious.' Iris stood up, took away the empty plates and brought cheese and a bowl of fresh fruit to the table. There was something faintly evasive about her manner which, had she felt less tired and stressed, Melissa would have challenged. As it was, she let the whole subject drop and they ate their fruit and cheese in virtual silence.

'Coffee?' offered Iris, folding her napkin.

'No thanks, it'll keep me awake and I haven't been sleeping too well just lately.'

'Herbal tea then?'

'Thanks, that might help.'

Iris yawned as she filled the kettle. 'Think I could use an early night,' she said.

'Me too.'

When, a short while later, Melissa returned to her own cottage, she found a message from Ken Harris on her answering machine. His second assignment had been completed; he was tired, planning an early night and would be home by mid-day tomorrow. It was not yet ten o'clock and she toyed briefly with the idea of returning the call, then decided against it. She was close to exhaustion herself; the sensible thing to do was go straight to bed. She took a hot shower, read for half an hour before switching off her light and then, for the first time since the discovery of Martha's body, fell instantly into a dreamless sleep.

When she awoke it was almost eight o'clock and her bedroom curtains were fringed with daylight. Her first thought was one of surprise that she had slept so long and so soundly. She went to the window and looked out on a landscape washed clean by rain and sparkling in sunshine. Signs of spring were everywhere; birds darted to and fro carrying wisps of nesting material, catkins bobbed in the breeze and buds swelled green in the hedgerows. When she opened the window to breathe in the cool, clean air, she heard the tremulous bleating of early lambs from the other side of the valley. Yesterday, she had been bowed down under thoughts of death and despair; this morning, with evidence of rebirth all around, the burden seemed to have slipped away.

Saturday's post had brought a letter from Mrs Grantley-Newcombe, expressing gratitude for agreeing to undertake the organisation of the Nearly New sale in aid of the Friends of Stowbridge Hospital, scheduled for mid-April.

Enclosed with the letter was a list of names and telephone numbers of ladies who, in previous years, had turned out their wardrobes in support of the cause. *It would be really, really kind*, Mrs Grantley-Newcombe had written, *if you could arrange to pick up their contributions and bring them to my house to be sorted and priced. It really, really is most* awfully *good of you to take this on at* such *short notice. I'm really, really grateful.*

Melissa re-read the letter as she ate her breakfast of cereal, toast and coffee, smiling a little at the fulsome language. She was looking forward to meeting the writer, of whom Gloria, despite not having personal knowledge, had given her such a vivid picture. She glanced at the clock; it was gone nine and most countrywomen were early risers. She finished her breakfast, cleared the table and sat down with the telephone.

She had just made her final call when Iris knocked at the door.

'How did you sleep?' she asked as she followed Melissa into the kitchen.

'Like a baby. Your herbal tea did the trick.'

'Thought it would. What've you got there?' Iris jabbed a forefinger at the list of names, each one now marked with a tick.

Melissa explained. 'It's Alice Hamley's idea of therapy, but she did it so diplomatically I couldn't refuse.'

Iris picked up the sheet of paper. 'Know most of these. Sold pictures to them.' She ran her eye down the list, commenting on each one that she recognised. 'Should get some decent togs from Joanna Vowden. Spends a fortune at Harvey Nichols. Lady Sugden dresses like a model so should be good for some bargains. Dulcie Bridgton looks like a horse and wears harness . . .'

'She what?'

'Leather gear with straps and things.' Iris continued her recital, finishing with, 'Mrs Bonnet. Don't know her.'

'That's pronounced Bone-*ay*,' Melissa informed her in an artificially refined accent. 'Very up-market and condescending. She didn't exactly *say* she thinks Mrs Grantley-Newcombe is a vulgar parvenue, but her tone when I mentioned the name was disparaging, to say the least.'

'Probably a parvenue herself. They're the worst snobs,' said Iris with feeling.

'Oh, she was quite gracious once we got talking, and she's promised me lots of *very good quality* clothes.' Melissa gave a wry smile as a thought struck her. 'I wonder how she'd react if she knew she was talking to the daughter of a small-town shopkeeper who'd been cast out for getting pregnant without benefit of clergy.'

'Probably forgive the lapse but not the humble origins.' Iris went to the window and stood looking out. 'Hope this weather lasts. Want to get started on the garden.' There was a pause; then she said, still with her back to Melissa, 'Heard from Ken yet?'

'Not yet. He'll probably call when he gets back to Cheltenham. Why do you ask?'

'Just wondered.' She swung round and made for the door. 'Mustn't hang around chatting. Got work to do.'

At around mid-day, Harris called Melissa to say he was back in the office. He had reports to write and would probably have to work late, so it was arranged that they would meet for dinner the following evening.

Just before he rang off, he said, 'By the way, have you seen today's *Gazette*?'

'Not yet. We don't get the early edition here. Why?'

'There's a bit about the Thanebury killings. Hang on, I'll read it to you.' There was a rustling sound as he turned the pages of the newspaper. 'Here we are. "A man, who has not been named but is believed to be a resident of Thanebury, was taken to Stowbridge Police Station last night and is helping police with their enquiries into the recent spate of murders in the village." Would you care to guess who that is?'

Melissa's skin broke out in gooseflesh as she said, 'Aggs, I suppose?'

'That's who my money's on. I'll try and get a word with Waters before I see you. Cheers.'

It probably was Aggs. He was known to have been out and about on at least three of the four fateful nights; he was known to have been carrying in his pocket 'something that could only have belonged to a woman'. Mrs Aggs had asked if there was anything unusual about Martha's body, which suggested that she knew about the Smiler's gruesome trade mark. If the 'something' had been a lipstick, it would explain her anxiety.

Of course, there was always the possibility that she had invented the whole story for some obscure reason of her own. Yet her relief on learning that another murder had been committed on a night when her husband had not left his bed had appeared wholly genuine.

Yes, it must be Aggs who was helping with enquiries. So why was it that another name had come simultaneously to mind?

Chapter Twelve

After lunching on a bowl of soup and some cheese, Melissa settled down to write an overdue letter to her son Simon, who had recently moved to New York following a three-year spell in Texas working for an oil company. Normally they spoke on the telephone once a month and alternated the calls with letters describing the minutiae of their daily lives. Simon's tended to be on the scrappy side; as his mother had often informed him, he had not inherited her literary talent, but he did have a knack of describing odd events with a quirky sense of humour that gave her much enjoyment. In turn, she regaled him with titbits of news and gossip from Upper Benbury.

Today, she covered several sheets of airmail paper with accounts of the party given by Madeleine and Dudley Ford, her meeting with the Donovans and the tragedy that lay behind their move to Gloucestershire, Iris's return from France and the progress of Harris Investigations. The words flowed easily from her pen; she chuckled aloud as she pictured his reaction to her recent involvement with the Friends of Stowbridge Hospital and the clutch of new characters she would soon be meeting. *More suspects in Nathan Latimer's next case, do I hear you say*? she wrote. She decided not to mention that she had half a mind to ditch her celebrated fictional detective; she had not yet clarified her own thoughts on the matter, nor discussed it with either her editor or Joe Martin, her agent.

She sat nibbling her pen for some time before adding a final paragraph:

> *I have to end with a piece of very sad news. Poor old Martha Willis died in her sleep the night before the Fords' party. I was the one who found her, which was a bit of a shock, but luckily Ken was with me and he took charge.*

There was no point in going into the horrific details; Simon would only worry and in any case she couldn't face reliving the experience. She signed the letter and sealed it, then put on her coat and walked into the village to post it. When she got back she found a message on her answering machine, asking her to contact Harris Investigations as soon as possible.

'It's Mrs Aggs,' Tricia explained when she called back. 'She wants to talk to you again. She wanted me to give her your number, but I said I couldn't do that.'

'Have you any idea what it's about?'

'No, but she sounded upset.'

It wasn't difficult to guess the reason: Raymond Aggs had been arrested. Since his wife had confided her suspicions to Melissa and to no one else, it must be Melissa who had betrayed him to the police.

'I don't know if you feel like speaking to her,' Tricia was saying.

'I'll think about it.' Melissa jotted down the number Tricia gave her, then asked, 'Is Ken there?'

'No, he went to deliver a report to a client. He wanted to discuss it personally.'

'Any idea how long he'll be?'

'I'm afraid not. He was going on somewhere else.'

Melissa felt her stomach sinking as she put the phone down. Her instinct was to ignore the message, or at least to wait until she had a chance to discuss it with Ken Harris. In agreeing to the first meeting with Mrs Aggs, she had acted in good faith – and for the time being, set the distraught woman's mind at rest. It wasn't her fault things had turned out differently. There was no way she could have avoided reporting back to Ken. The contact had been made through him, and Mrs Aggs herself had triggered the enquiry by approaching Harris Investigations in the first place. If her resolution had not failed, if she had voiced her suspicions directly to the detective, the result would have been the same. So why should Melissa now be called upon to justify herself to an angry, possibly hysterical woman? If Aggs really was the Smiler, she would have to come to terms with it; there was nothing Melissa could do. And in any case, Ken had specifically warned her against becoming further involved.

But even as her mind concocted this apologia, she knew that what lay behind it was moral cowardice. The very thing that Mrs Aggs dreaded had come to pass and she, Melissa Craig, with the best of intentions, had been instrumental in bringing it about. The least she could do now was respond to this second cry for help, even if it meant listening to a storm of reproach. It might do something to relieve the poor woman's feelings. 'And since when,' Melissa said aloud as she reached for the telephone, 'have Ken's injunctions not to poke my nose into his cases ever held me back?'

The phone rang several times before it was answered. Eventually, a voice that she hardly recognised whispered, 'Hullo.'

'This is Melissa Craig. I believe . . .' she began, but got no further before Mrs Aggs broke in with a cry that was almost a sob.

'Oh, Mrs Craig! I've been praying you'd call. There's no one else . . . my neighbours . . . I can't show my face out of doors . . . I'm going out of my mind here alone and . . .' Distress made the following words unintelligible.

'Mrs Aggs, please don't cry,' Melissa entreated. 'I can't tell you how sorry I was when I heard about it.'

There was a muffled gasp from the other end of the wire, a moment of silence, and then, 'You've heard about it? How? How many other people know?' There was something like panic behind the final question.

'I can't really say . . . that is . . .' Melissa found herself floundering and she evaded the question by asking one of her own. 'When did it happen?'

'On Saturday. He . . .' Once again, emotion dammed the flow of words.

In a flash of insight, Melissa divined that Mrs Aggs' motive for wanting to speak to her was neither anger nor resentment, but a desperate need to confide in someone outside the close-knit community in which she lived, someone whose disapproving, possibly contemptuous gaze would not greet her every time she ventured out of her house. She was the type of woman for whom the good opinion of her neighbours was vital to her self-esteem. Melissa had a momentary recollection of her own mother's reaction to the news that her daughter had become pregnant outside marriage, heard once again over the years the impassioned cry of, 'You've disgraced us! How will I ever hold my head up again?' Mrs Aggs was not of her mother's generation, but she had the same attitude to that all important quality: respectability.

On impulse, Melissa said, 'Would you like me to come and see you? It might help you to talk about it face to face. The phone's pretty impersonal.'

'Would you?' The voice became stronger, like a fading signal returning. 'Would you really? I'd be so grateful. There's no one round here . . .'

'I could come now, if you like. I know the road to Thanebury; just tell me how to reach your house.'

'It's on the right, about two hundred yards past the church. You can park on our drive. Raymond won't be . . .' The signal faded again; this time it was Melissa's turn to interrupt.

'That's fine,' she said briskly. 'I'll be with you in half an hour or so.'

The village of Thanebury was reached along a narrow lane off the main road, at the bottom of a long, winding hill, so that travellers approaching from either direction viewed it from an altitude of several hundred feet. It had a compact, self-contained appearance, as if it had been set down in its finished state in the surrounding farmland and never touched since. All the houses and barns were of local stone, the tiled roofs speckled with lichen, the boundary walls overgrown with ivy and moss. The only building that appeared to be less than a hundred years old was the church, but that too had weathered, blended into the background and become part of the whole.

Briar Cottage was almost at the far end of the village. Following Mrs Aggs' directions, Melissa drove slowly along the main street. Several pedestrians exercising dogs or pushing prams pointedly turned their heads to watch her pass; she sensed invisible, suspicious eyes lurking behind every window. Outside a small general store, two women were deep in conversation; as she drew level, another emerged and joined them. In her mirror, she saw the little group staring after her and felt their mistrust and anxiety pursuing her until a curve in the road hid them from view.

As she parked the Golf on the drive of Briar Cottage, she saw a curtain move. The front door opened before she had time to ring the bell; Mrs Aggs beckoned her inside and then hastily stood back as if afraid of being seen by anyone else. Melissa reflected that there would be good reason to worry, once the press learned the identity of the suspect. It was a wonder they hadn't got on to it already; the rumours must be flying, even if no official announcement had been made.

'It's so good of you to come,' Mrs Aggs faltered. She had evidently been weeping; her nose and eyes were red and her grey hair lay back from her brow in furrows, as if agitated fingers had been repeatedly dragged through it. She closed the door and led the way into a tiny sitting-room, somewhat over-furnished but neat as a new pin. On a low table in front of the fire was a tray of tea-things. She pointed to a chair and said, 'Do sit down. The kettle's on the boil, I won't be a minute,' and bustled out.

Melissa sat in the high-backed wing chair upholstered in crimson velour, one of a pair placed on either side of the fireplace, and glanced round the room. There was a great deal of highly-polished wood and shining brass and copper reflected the firelight on the hearth. Porcelain ornaments were carefully arranged in a glass-fronted cabinet and spotless windows sparkled in the sunshine.

It was evident that Mrs Aggs was intensely house-proud. On the mantelpiece, symmetrically placed on either side of an old-fashioned wooden clock, were two photographs, one of a bridal couple, the other of a pretty, solemn-faced little girl. Melissa stood up to take a closer look. The bride was unmistakably a young – and surprisingly attractive – Mrs Aggs; the child bore a striking resemblance to the groom.

'Yes, that is my . . . our wedding photograph,' said a voice behind her.

She swung round, startled and embarrassed. 'Forgive me for being inquisitive,' she apologised.

'That's all right. I often look at it myself and wonder if I ever really looked like that.'

Melissa tried to think of some comment that would not sound banal, but failed. Instead she pointed to the second photograph. 'Is this your daughter?'

'Yes, that's our little Sheila. We lost her a month after that was taken. She ran out into the road behind the school bus and a car knocked her over.' The words were spoken lifelessly, as if some part of the mother had died with the child.

Melissa felt an overwhelming sense of pity for the woman whose entire concentration appeared at that moment to be focused on pouring tea from a white china teapot patterned with roses into matching cups set out on an embroidered tray-cloth. Death had claimed her only child, time had robbed her of her looks and her husband was detained on suspicion of murder. She was alone, despairing and afraid, unable to face or confide in anyone but a woman whom she had met only once, yet to whom she had revealed her innermost fears.

She sat down opposite Melissa and sipped her tea. For

the moment, she had her emotions well in hand. 'Of course, it's bound to come out sooner or later . . . people will have to know,' she began, 'but I feel too ashamed, too embarrassed to face any of my neighbours just yet. At the same time, I was desperate to talk to someone . . . I tried to contact the vicar but he's out, he's got several parishes to look after . . . and you were so kind. I do hope you understand.'

'Then you're not angry with me?'

'Angry with you?' Mrs Aggs' colourless eyebrows lifted in surprise. 'Why should I be?'

'I assumed you thought I was the one who put the police on to your husband.'

'The police?' Mrs Aggs looked even more bewildered. 'What have they got to do with Raymond leaving me for another woman?'

'Your husband has left you? Is that why . . . ?' It began to dawn on Melissa that she had made a fearful blunder. 'I had no idea.'

'But you said . . . I mean, I had the impression that you knew. I wondered who could have told you.'

Melissa put down her half-finished cup of tea and began nervously fiddling with her wrist-watch. 'I'm afraid I got hold of the wrong end of the stick,' she said. 'You see, Ken – Mr Harris – told me a man from Thanebury had been detained for questioning about the murders and we both thought it must be your husband.'

'But we'd already established . . .'

'That he couldn't have killed Martha Willis? Yes, I know. But Ken said there might be a copycat murderer at work, that it wasn't certain that whoever killed the people in Thanebury was the same person who killed Martha.'

Mrs Aggs looked aghast. Her cup rattled on its saucer

and she put it down with a shaking hand. 'In other words, he thought Raymond could still be the Smiler?'

'The . . . who?'

'Here in Thanebury we call him the Smiler. Oh, we know all about what he does to his victims after he's smothered them. We don't talk about it – the police asked us not to but we wouldn't anyway, Thanebury people keep themselves to themselves – but we know. We all know.' There was something about her expression that made Melissa feel uncomfortable; behind the unprepossessing exterior, a keen intelligence was at work. When she spoke again, she seemed to be thinking aloud. 'So, you told your friend Mr Harris – who is, if I remember correctly, an ex-policeman – what I told you? And I suppose he talked to his former colleagues?'

'I imagine so.' Melissa decided not to mention that a serving officer had actually taken part in the discussion.

'I wonder . . .' Mrs Aggs stared into the fire. In its glow, her features appeared softer, less gaunt, revealing a glimpse of the woman she had once been. After several minutes of silence she turned back to Melissa and said, in a weary, resigned voice, 'I'm beginning to understand. He accused me of not trusting him, of "stirring things up" as he put it.'

'Did you tell him what you really suspected him of?'

'Oh, no!' Mrs Aggs winced, as if the memory aroused by the question had caused physical pain.

'How did you find out about the affair?'

'That's the stupid part of it, I didn't. He told me. He came home one day in a towering rage, making wild accusations, saying I'd been checking up on him. The way he blurted it out, he made it seem as if the whole thing was my fault. It was so unjust – I know I'd been suspicious, but I hadn't said a word to anyone but you. After what you told me, I decided to believe his story and forget all about it.' Mrs Aggs gave a short, bitter laugh. 'It's ironic, isn't it? When I went to Harris Investigations I was only pretending I suspected him of being unfaithful. What I was really afraid of was so much worse that I could hardly think rationally. I suppose I should be thankful, shouldn't I, that it was only his affair with his secretary that was, to use his own words, tearing him apart, making him lose sleep? That's why he kept going out at night. To try and think what to do. Now he's left me to live with her. Oh, dear God! Why didn't I leave well alone?' She covered her face with her hands and wept silently for a few moments.

'I feel badly about it too,' Melissa said miserably. 'If I hadn't betrayed your confidence, this would never have happened.'

'It's not your fault.' Mrs Aggs dried her eyes with her handkerchief and put out a hand. 'I knew there was something wrong . . . it would have come out sooner or later.'

'I suppose so,' said Melissa with a sigh. Then something else struck her. 'When was the last time you saw your husband?' she asked.

'On Saturday night, when he left.'

'What time was that?'

'It must have been nearly midnight. We had a dreadful argument that seemed to go on for ever. Then he went upstairs, packed a suitcase and left.'

'And you haven't heard from him since?' It had occurred to Melissa that Raymond Aggs could still be the suspect referred to in the newspaper report, but the reply to her question made it seem unlikely.

'He phoned from the office this morning, saying he'd be back for the rest of his things at the weekend. He suggested I might like to be out when he came, "to save unpleasantness, out of consideration for my feelings".'

'Consideration for his own feelings is more like it,' said Melissa scornfully. 'It seems to me he's behaved abominably . . . and if anyone should be feeling ashamed, it's him, not you,' she added, thinking that a little anger might not be a bad thing.

'You're right.' Mrs Aggs lifted her head and straightened her back. 'I've been a good wife to him and if this is how he treats me, then he's not worth crying over. Just the same,' despite her brave resolve, her eyes were swimming again, 'I find it so hard to believe . . . he's always been so upright, so God-fearing . . . how could he do it?'

'I'm afraid it's a question a lot of wives have to ask themselves,' said Melissa. 'Put it down to a mid-life crisis. It may not last,' she added, trying to sound encouraging.

'You mean, he might come back to me? I'm not sure that I'd want him, knowing he'd been . . . with another woman. I suppose,' – dull colour crept into the wan cheeks – 'I was never very good at . . . that sort of thing . . . you know what I mean? Perhaps it's partly my fault.'

'You mustn't blame yourself,' said Melissa earnestly, 'and don't go hiding away like a criminal. You haven't done anything shameful.'

'Thank you, Mrs Craig, thank you very much for being so sympathetic and understanding.'

'I'm glad I've been able to help.' Seeing an opportunity to end her visit, Melissa got to her feet. She took one of her business cards from her handbag and held it out. 'Here's my telephone number. Give me a call if you feel like having a chat. And . . . why don't you call me Melissa?'

'Thank you Melissa. My name's Bertha. Not very pretty is it? Like me.' She gave a rueful smile and patted ineffectively at her disarranged hair.

At the door, Melissa asked, 'How long has Mr Jarman been your vicar?'

'Just under a year. Do you know him?'

'I met him when he called on our rector, and my friends and I came to yesterday's memorial service. Is he popular in the parish?'

Bertha Aggs showed no surprise at the question. 'It took us a while to get used to him,' she said, 'but he's a very caring, conscientious man. Rather flamboyant in his manner and perhaps a little too much given to harping on the after life – but I suppose, with an ageing population, that's what most of us ought to be thinking about anyway.' A faint smile suggested that she was not entirely lacking a sense of humour. 'He certainly shows a great deal of concern for the sick and dying,' she added, her expression once more serious. 'And he's been a tower of strength during this terrible time. The authorities wanted to send in what they called "trauma counsellors", but no one was interested. Mr Jarman has given us all the support we need.' The spontaneous tribute was spoken with apparent sincerity, but with no particular warmth. Perhaps Bertha Aggs was anxious not to appear too much under the priest's charismatic spell.

Keeping her tone casual, Melissa remarked, 'I believe he has a particular appeal for young people as well?'

'Oh yes, he certainly has a way with them. He holds special services for them once a month. Guitar music and dancing in the aisles, I'm told. It seems strange to people of my generation, but if it brings the young people into the church I suppose it's a good thing. The girls especially think the world of him – they'll do anything he asks. It seems unnatural to me, the way they dote on the man.' For the moment, Bertha seemed to forget her own troubles in her concern for the Reverend Jarman's young acolytes. 'In my opinion,' she asserted, 'they should be having fun with their college friends, not spending all their free time doing good works at his bidding.'

'It's a bit unusual, but it's better than getting into mischief,' Melissa remarked. She held out a hand. 'Well, good bye for now, Bertha.'

'Good bye Melissa, and once again, thank you.'

Driving back through the village, Melissa met a car coming from the opposite direction. The road was narrow and both cars had to slow down; as they drew level, Melissa recognised the driver as the young man she had seen with Laura Maddox in the multi-storey car park in Cheltenham. Seated in the front passenger seat was the Reverend Gareth Jarman.

On the news that evening it was announced that a man who had been questioned by police in connection with the Thanebury murders had been released without charge.

Chapter Thirteen

The first thing Ken Harris said when he arrived at Hawthorn Cottage on Tuesday evening was, 'It wasn't Aggs, it was the local padre, and they've had to let him go.'

Melissa took his coat and hung it up in the tiny hallway. 'So what else is new?' she asked smugly.

He shot her a look of surprise mingled with disappointment, like a humorist hearing the punch line of his best joke delivered by someone else. 'How the hell did you know?'

'I went to see Bertha Aggs. On the way back I met the car bringing Mr Jarman home.'

'He was sent home in a patrol car? Isn't that typical of Holloway?' His voice held a hint of a sneer. Evidently, ex-Chief Inspector Harris was still smarting at being snubbed by a former junior colleague after the discovery of Martha Willis's body. 'It'll be all over Thanebury by now that their vicar's under suspicion.'

'I'm afraid you can't blame Holloway this time,' said Melissa. 'It was an unmarked car. I guessed where he'd been because I recognised the driver.' She told him about her encounter with Laura Maddox and the young companion who was so obviously besotted with her. 'She called him Cliffie, her favourite little copper, and promised to give him better grub than he gets in the police canteen.'

Ken gave a soft whistle. 'So that's what the young fool's up to – playing the toy boy.'

'You know him?'

'Clifford Fenn, one of the most promising lads we've recruited for a long time.' The 'we' did not escape Melissa. Out of the Force for a year or more but still identifying with them, she thought. 'He was made a detective constable just before I left and he was doing really well,' Ken went on, 'but Matt Waters told me recently they're a bit concerned about him. They know he's been dating someone pretty regularly – someone he seems very keen on – but he's been so cagey, they thought she must be married.'

'Not married, just old enough to be his mother.'

Ken shook his head in disapproval. 'The Super's not going to like it.'

'Does he have to know?'

'I'll mention it to Waters. It'll be up to him then.'

Melissa was about to add that Clifford Fenn had apparently undertaken to carry out some task for Laura which she suspected of being not quite above-board, but changed her mind. Nothing had been said to suggest that it had anything to do with his job. Whatever line officialdom might take, his private life was, in her opinion, his own business so long as his work was unaffected by it. She hoped she had not caused problems for him; instinct told her that he would have enough to face up to when his romantic dream ended, as it surely would when Laura tired of him.

Ken wandered into the sitting-room and sat down with the relaxed air of one entirely at home in his surroundings.

'I've booked our table for seven-thirty,' he said. 'Can you be ready in half an hour?'

'What do you mean?' She feigned indignation. 'I only have to put my coat on – if I don't look glamorous enough for you, you'd better find another date.'

'Don't be so touchy.' He leaned forward and grabbed her by the hand. 'Come here and let me look at you.' His appraising glance travelled from head to foot and back again. 'You look great,' he said softly and tried to pull her towards him, but she resisted. 'Not now, you'll smudge my make-up,' she protested, releasing her hand. 'Can I get you a drink?'

'I'd love a beer.'

She fetched it, handed it to him and sat down. 'Tell me more about the Reverend Jarman,' she said. 'What made Holloway pull him in, and why did he let him go?'

'It seems he and Mellor attended the memorial service for the Smiler's victims on Sunday. I understand it included prayers for Martha Willis, by the way.'

'I know, I was there. I went with Iris and Genty Donovan, but I never spotted any policemen.'

'They were probably skulking at the back of the church. Anyway, there was something about the reverend gentleman that roused Holloway's suspicions, so they called at the vicarage after the service. He'd been interviewed before, of course, during house to house enquiries, but this time it seems he became hostile, quite stroppy in fact, so they took him to the nick.'

'There *is* something odd about him,' said Melissa thoughtfully. 'In fact, he gives me the shivers. He seems obsessed with death and the after life and bangs on about eternal bliss. And he's got this little band of teenage girls running around doing good works in the parish. He calls them his "Daughters of Light".'

'There's nothing wrong with that, surely?'

'It's the effect he has on them that bothers me. Bertha Aggs says they've all got crushes on him, except for Natalie, who found the third body and looks more scared than adoring. I don't think he's a healthy influence at all, and neither does Bertha.'

To her chagrin, Melissa realised that she was trembling; before she could stop herself she was pouring out the sick fancies that had all but taken possession of her during the Reverend Jarman's address. Ken was full of concern.

'Darling, you should have called me and I'd have come right away.'

'I thought about it, but I didn't find your message until gone ten, and you sounded so tired, I didn't want to disturb you. Besides, it seemed such a load of tripe when I thought about it afterwards, but at the time . . . it was that mouth, that awful red, smiling mouth . . . I could still see it.'

'That's only natural.' He was squatting beside her, holding both her hands, completely enveloping them in his own. 'It's going to take time to get over it.'

'I feel better for telling you.'

'That's good.' He sat back on his own chair. 'Here's something to make you feel better still. It was partly your doing that Holloway began suspecting Jarman.'

'How so?'

'Matt Waters passed on your idea that the Smiler could be a religious fanatic. That set him thinking.'

'Clever old me!' She gave a shaky laugh. 'But presumably Jarman's been eliminated now?'

'Not by any means. He hasn't an alibi for any of the nights in question and he visited all the victims regularly so he knew their habits, where they kept their keys and so on. He could easily have got into their houses during the night without leaving any clues. Holloway got a warrant to search the vicarage, but nothing incriminating was found, so there was no way they could hold him.'

'By "nothing incriminating" I take it you mean, no lipstick?'

'That was the obvious thing to look for.'

'Which reminds me, have you heard the latest about Raymond Aggs?'

'Only that whatever it was his wife found in his pocket that started all the rumpus – presumably a lipstick – must have belonged to his girlfriend. He's been having an affair with a woman in his office for some time, hence the sleepless nights – all down to tussles with his conscience, he claims.'

'Do you suppose he realises he's a suspect?'

Ken grinned. 'I understand not. He thinks the chap Holloway sent to check up on him is a private eye employed by his wife. He had a few unkind things to say about her. You said you'd been to see her – does she know?'

'I'll say she knows – the poor woman's devastated. He's left her and moved in with the girlfriend.' Melissa related the details of her visit to Thanebury. 'There's an atmosphere in that village that you could cut with a knife,' she added. 'You feel it simply by driving through; people look suspiciously at every passing stranger.'

'You can't wonder at it. It must be a very uncomfortable place to live in just now, with everyone wondering whether their next-door neighbour is the Smiler.'

'The locals call him that too. They all know about the business with the lipstick.'

'I guessed as much, and if you remember, so did Matt.'

'I suppose it's got to be someone local, hasn't it? Unless . . . supposing someone's been gossiping to outsiders about what goes on in the village?'

'Thanebury people don't gossip. Matt says they've had the devil of a job to get them to say anything except what lovely old dears the victims were.'

'The older folk might be like that, but what about the youngsters? The "Daughters of Light", for example. At least one of them is a student and the others certainly looked as if they were. Young people chatter away to their peers about all sorts of things – they're almost certain to have spoken about their dishy vicar and the "good works" he encourages them to do. They might have repeated all that stuff about "eternal bliss" and the joys of the after-life that he keeps ramming down their throats.'

'You're not suggesting the Smiler is a young person?'

'No, but someone might have overheard them talking . . . someone mentally unstable who thinks the old and lonely should be quietly put out of their misery.'

Harris considered, his features creased in a frown. 'It's possible, I suppose, but unlikely – the Smiler's got to be someone with intimate local knowledge. I'll pass on the suggestion for what it's worth – I know the Super's tearing his hair out in desperation for anything like a lead and the media are getting restless because of the lack of progress.'

'He still hasn't told them about the smile?'

'No, but my guess is he'll have to pretty soon. They know he's hiding something.'

He finished his beer, stood up and began prowling round the room with his hands in his pockets. He looked up for a few moments at the ceiling, where exposed oak beams cleared his head by only a few inches. Then he stared into the fire glowing on the stone hearth before moving on to study the pictures on the whitewashed walls and the crowded bookshelves on either side of the chimney breast. Finally, he turned to look at Melissa, still seated in her chair but following him with her eyes.

'This is a lovely, peaceful room,' he said softly. 'In fact, the whole cottage has a peaceful atmosphere.'

'That's exactly why I love it so much,' she replied. 'It's one of the reasons why I find it easy to work here . . . and why I can't bear the thought of leaving it.'

'I do understand that, but . . .' He seemed to be about to say something else, then broke off, glanced at the brass carriage clock on the mantelpiece and said abruptly, 'We'd better be going.'

Chapter Fourteen

The following day was the third in succession without rain. The temperature had been rising steadily and when Melissa opened her bedroom window the morning air flowed softly over her head and shoulders like a veil of silk. She washed, dressed and hurried downstairs, determined not to waste a moment of what promised to be a perfect day for tackling the garden.

Gloria arrived at nine o'clock. She bounced in like a burst of spring sunshine herself, blond curls framing pink cheeks, warm brown eyes aglow with health and good humour.

'My, what a smashing morning!' she exclaimed as she peeled off her jacket, tied on her apron and rolled up her sleeves. 'I seen Miss Ash hard at it in her garden already. Amazing for her age, she be.'

'She's only in her fifties,' Melissa pointed out.

'Yeah, well, that's quite old, innit?' Gloria was barely thirty and in the bloom of fecund womanhood.

'It's all relative, though,' said Melissa, thinking with inward amusement that she too was probably written off in the younger woman's mind as more or less over the hill. 'I mean, to someone who's only eighteen, thirty probably sounds middle-aged.'

'S'pose so.' Not a whit abashed, Gloria went to the

cupboard where she kept her cleaning materials. 'Talking of teenagers,' she said when she emerged with the vacuum cleaner and a plastic bucket containing an assortment of dusters and polishes, 'you remembers that student at the art college what I told you about?'

'The one who discovered one of the murder victims in Thanebury?'

'Thassright.'

'I remember.' That would be Natalie, of course. 'What about her?'

'Tried to top herself.'

'Good heavens, when?'

'Dunno exactly. It were on Cotswold Sound radio this morning.'

'Is she going to be all right?'

'Guess so. Her Mum found her passed out with an empty pill bottle beside her and called an ambulance.'

'Poor girl.' Melissa's mind flew back to the scene in Thanebury church on Sunday evening. She recalled noticing something akin to terror on the girl's face during the Reverend Jarman's address, her pleading expression as she turned towards Genty . . . and how her friends had hustled her away. Was it simply the trauma of finding the body that had affected Natalie so profoundly, or was it some knowledge too terrible to speak of that had made her try to end her own life?

It was possible that Acting DCI Holloway and Sergeant Mellor had witnessed that little episode in the church; if so, what had they made of it? Had Ken Harris passed on to Sergeant Waters, or to one of his other contacts in the police, Melissa's misgivings about the influence of the charismatic priest on his so-called 'Daughters of Light'? The latest twist to the tragedy seemed to give added significance to their devotion to him. Her mind ran on, exploring the possibilities it opened up. What if the girls knew – or suspected – that he was the killer? Under his mesmeric spell, they might delude themselves into believing that he had a divine mission to release the elderly victims from earthly tribulation and allow them to enter into what he kept referring to as 'eternal bliss'. Fanatically devoted to him, they would say nothing. He would feel secure in the knowledge that they would never betray him . . . but suppose Natalie had begun to crack? According to Gloria – and confirmed by Genty – she had become withdrawn since her ordeal, barely speaking; 'just sits in a corner drawing pictures', Gloria had said. Was it the weight of a dreadful secret that had brought her to this?

On reflection, it was possible that some good might come out of this pitiful gesture. Once in the care of experts, Natalie might be persuaded to talk openly about her experience and so relieve the pent-up torment. Little by little, she might reveal what she knew . . . it was at this point that Melissa felt a premonition that the girl might be in danger. Supposing what she said was liable to incriminate someone? It would be in that person's interests that she should not recover from the overdose. As soon as Gloria was out of earshot, Melissa flew to the telephone and called Harris Investigations.

Ken's reaction was at once disappointing and reassuring. 'I told you, the Super and his team haven't written Jarman out of the frame yet, and I'm sure they're taking the girl's suicide attempt very seriously,' he said after she had told him of her fears. 'There's almost certainly a specially trained woman detective at the hospital, waiting to interview her as soon as the doctors will allow.'

'There should be a police guard with her all the time,' Melissa insisted, 'and the police should be warned about all that "Daughters of Light" rubbish . . . suppose Jarman tries to shut her up for good?'

'For heaven's sake, Mel, give the police some credit,' Harris said impatiently. 'They haven't been twiddling their thumbs all this time – do you suppose that hasn't occurred to them? She's in good hands, never fear. Just leave it to them. Now, you must excuse me, I've an appointment. I'll see you at the weekend. Good bye for now.' Without waiting for her to respond, he hung up.

Melissa put down the receiver feeling deflated. Well, she had done what she could. Ken was right, of course – the police weren't fools. Upstairs, the vacuum was humming and above it, Gloria was giving a hearty rendering of the latest hit by Madonna. Outside, the sunshine beckoned. 'To work,' she told herself and went to find her gardening clothes.

As Gloria had said, Iris was already out there, energetically digging, weeding and clearing the detritus of winter. Melissa beckoned her to the fence that divided their gardens and told her about Natalie.

'Poor kid!' said Iris, looking shocked. 'Must have been in a worse state than they thought. Hope she'll pull through.'

'Gloria seemed to think her mother found her in time. Iris, I'm so frightened for her. I told Ken and he's sure everything's under control, but . . .'

'He's right. Police know their business. Stop worrying and get on with clearing that up.' Iris gestured with her weeding fork towards Melissa's neglected garden before going back to her own task of pruning shrubs. Over her shoulder, she added, 'Come for lunch.'

'Thanks, love to.'

A good spell of digging soon got Melissa's circulation going and her lungs happily pumping oxygen round her system. When Gloria had departed, she scrubbed the dirt from her hands, changed her shoes and went next door. Over spicy lentil soup and crusty home-baked rolls, the two friends discussed the latest development in the hunt for the Smiler.

'Those girls know something, I'm sure of it,' said Melissa. 'I reckon they suspect Jarman and they're so besotted by him they'd die on the rack rather than betray him. Of course,' she stopped in the act of putting a piece of bread in her mouth, 'that's why they wouldn't let Natalie talk to Genty on Sunday. They were terrified she'd give something away.'

'You could be right,' Iris agreed. She put the empty soup bowls in the sink and brought fruit and cheese to the table. 'Does Genty know about the kid trying to top herself?'

'I've no idea. Perhaps I'll pop round and see her after lunch. I've a feeling she's at home on Wednesdays; she only lectures part-time at the art college.'

Genty was alone in the house when Melissa called.

'Sirry's taken Father to see his consultant,' she explained as she held the door open for her visitor to enter.

'How is he doing?'

Genty shrugged. 'There isn't much permanent progress, although he does cheer up when Iris comes to see him.'

'I didn't know she'd been again.'

'She's called round a couple of times. Once, she even made him laugh – it was magical. The sad thing is, half an hour after she's gone, he's back where he was.'

'Knowing Iris, she'll persevere.'

'Fancy her saying nothing to you.'

'That's Iris all over.' Melissa felt a rush of affectionate pride towards her friend. 'She never talks about her good deeds.'

'Sirry and I have become very fond of her. Look, I was just making some coffee. Would you like some?'

'No thanks, but you go ahead with yours.' Melissa followed her into the kitchen and perched on a stool. 'Actually, I've come with some rather serious news about Natalie.' Briefly, she related all she knew.

'That's awful, simply awful!' Genty exclaimed. 'I knew, of course, what a dreadful effect finding poor Miss Twigg had on her, but I never thought . . . you know, I was almost the only person at college that she spoke to after it happened.'

'What did she say?'

'Not much, only that it was dreadful and she dreamed about it every night. She didn't miss any of my classes, but I don't think she took in a word I was saying. She used to sit at the back of the room, doodling on a sketch pad.'

'Drawing pictures, my cleaning lady said. She knows someone who works at the art college,' Melissa added in response to Genty's look of surprise. 'It's amazing, isn't it, how these things get around? I don't suppose,' she added after a moment's thought, 'Natalie ever showed you her drawings?'

Genty shook her head. 'No, never. She wouldn't let anyone see them.'

'That's a pity. They might have given some sort of clue.'

'Clue to what?'

'To the identity of the killer. I believe she may know, or suspect, who it is.'

'Do you think so? It's possible of course, but surely she'd have said . . .' Genty frowned and began fiddling with the cafetière, her expression thoughtful. For several moments she said nothing; then glancing up and catching Melissa's eye, she said apologetically, 'Students do sometimes doodle during lectures, I'm afraid. It usually means they aren't paying attention. It never occurred to me that what Natalie was drawing might be significant.' She poured coffee into a mug, still frowning.

'It was just an idea.'

'I wonder if she's well enough to have visitors? I feel in a way responsible . . . perhaps I should have tried harder to get her to talk, but she always shut up like an oyster whenever I . . .' Genty broke off and waved the cafetière in Melissa's direction. 'Are you sure you wouldn't like some?'

'Quite sure, thanks. Look, you mustn't blame yourself.' As she spoke, Melissa remembered saying exactly the same words to Bertha Aggs. Such a glib little phrase . . . but was it true? Could one ever claim to be completely guiltless in such a situation? With hindsight, wasn't there always a lingering feeling that one could have done *something* to avert a tragedy? Aloud she went on, 'Natalie should have had professional counselling from the start. I'm told it was on offer, but no one took it up. At least, now, she'll be interviewed by experts as soon as she's well enough. I'm sure she'd love to see you, if the doctors will allow it.'

'Do you know what hospital she's in?'

'Stowbridge General, I imagine. Why don't you call them and ask?'

'I think I will. Thank you, Melissa, for telling me.'

Chapter Fifteen

On Thursday morning, Melissa received a telephone call from Mrs Dorinda Grantley-Newcombe, enquiring about progress with the preparations for the forthcoming 'Nearly New' sale in aid of the Friends of Stowbridge Hospital. Melissa assured her that the matter was well in hand and that it was her intention that very morning to contact all the generous ladies who had promised contributions of clothing. An almost palpable gush of gratitude swept along the wire.

'It's *reelly*, *reelly* kind of you to take this on at such short notice,' said Mrs Grantley-Newcombe. 'I was wondering if we could arrange a time . . . I mean, would it be too much to ask you to bring the things to my house and help me to sort and price them? I've never done this before, and I'm not at all sure . . .'

'I'll deliver them, of course – I was planning to anyway – but I don't know any more than you about what prices to charge. What about your committee? Some of them must have been involved before.'

'Oh, *them!*' A mixture of exasperation and disparagement crept into Mrs Grantley-Newcombe's voice, which held an underlying trace of nasality typical of the Home Counties – very different from the warm, rounded vowels of Gloucestershire and certainly not the exaggerated form of standard English affected by certain members of the landed gentry. It reminded Melissa of another voice that she had recently heard, but could not remember where.

'I'm afraid the committee haven't been terribly helpful,' her caller continued, somewhat peevishly. 'Not mentioning any names, of course, but they do make me feel a bit of an outsider, just because my family hasn't lived in the county for hundreds of years.'

'Oh, I'm sure they don't mean to.' Melissa did her best to sound reassuring, although she was well aware of the stand-offish attitude certain people tended to adopt towards those they considered their social inferiors. 'Anyway, I'm hoping to collect some things today; perhaps I could bring them to your house tomorrow morning? Would that be convenient?'

'Of course it would. I'm *reelly*, *reelly* grateful to you.'

'That's quite all right. I'll see you tomorrow, then.'

Mrs Grantley-Newcombe rang off and Melissa settled down to make her own calls. She was in luck; almost every one of the ladies whose names were on her list had kept her promise to turn out her wardrobe, and in each case someone would be at home that morning to hand over her contributions. Armed with her list of addresses and a map – a number of the ladies lived in villages scattered around Stowbridge – she put on her outdoor things and went to get the car out of the garage. Iris, who was putting empty milk bottles in her porch, looked across and waved.

'Hullo!' she called. 'Where are you off to?' When told of the proposed visit to Carston Manor next day, she said, 'Give you a hand if you like.'

'That's kind of you, Iris. I'm sure Mrs Grantley-Newcombe will be very appreciative.'

'Like to see what she's done with the place. Eighteenth century, some of it. Maybe she'll commission a painting.'

'You never know. See you later, then.' Iris went back indoors and Melissa set off on her errand.

She returned some time later with the back seat and the boot of the Golf crammed with bags of clothing. Iris, who was digging in her vegetable patch, immediately dropped her fork, shed her gardening gloves and came to help unload the collection. Once indoors, she pounced on an elegant, dark green and gold plastic carrier. 'This from Joanna Vowden? Don't tell me she's abandoned Harvey Nichols for Harrods?'

'No, that lot is from Mrs Bonnet, pronounced Bone-*ay*,' said Melissa with a grin. 'My God, what a snob that woman is! From the way she looked down her over-powdered nose at the mention of Mrs Grantley-Newcombe, you'd think the poor woman was lower than her own servants. She made fun of her accent and said she was "trying to make out she's a lady". Beat that for cattiness.'

'She the one who promised "very good quality" clothes?' enquired Iris, rummaging in the Harrods bag.

'That's right. What has she given us?'

Iris pulled out a number of garments, inspected the labels and held out a woollen sweater. 'All from the same very good quality chain store, and some of 'em could do with a wash,' she said disdainfully.

'I think,' said Melissa, when they had finished sorting the contents of the bags, 'that I'm going to like Mrs Grantley-Newcombe more than some of the people who patronise her.'

'Me too,' Iris agreed. 'Bet she's much nicer than stuck-up old Mother Bonnet.'

'Pronounced Bone-*ay*!' corrected Melissa in her best high society voice. 'Come on, let's have some lunch.'

Over toasted cheese sandwiches in the kitchen they discussed the latest news – or rather, in the case of the hunt for Martha Willis's killer, the lack of it.

'The police seem pretty certain that the Thanebury killings were all carried out by the Smiler,' said Melissa, 'but there's a question mark hanging over Martha. Her death is still very much on everyone's mind. Every time I go into Mrs Foster's shop, someone in there is talking about it.'

'Dudley Ford been on to you about locking doors and so on?'

Melissa rolled her eyes to the ceiling. 'Tell me about it! You know, I think he's rather enjoying the situation. He's been to every house in the village, haranguing people about security and ticking off anyone who's left so much as a window open.'

'Encouraging a siege mentality. Thinks he's back in the army, giving orders to his troops.' Iris gave a mischievous smile. 'Don't think you and I need worry, Mel – not old or decrepit enough to interest the Smiler. Dudley should keep an eye on Madeleine, though,' she added, with a flash of malice in her eyes.

'Now *you're* being catty!'

'What about Natalie?' asked Iris, ignoring the reproof. 'Heard if she's well enough to be questioned yet?'

'I spoke to Sirry Donovan this morning and she said Genty called the hospital yesterday evening, but no one would tell her anything.'

'That figures. The fuzz have probably warned the authorities to keep stumm.'

'I hear you've been to see Cluny again. How did you find him?'

'Hard to say.'

'Meaning?'

'He see-saws . . . one minute, talkative, even laughing. Then he sort of switches off.'

'Still brooding over his son's death, I suppose,' said Melissa thoughtfully. 'I wonder if he's suffering from guilt feelings.'

'Why should he?'

'Cluny's a perfectionist. Perhaps he put too much pressure on Saxe – all that talk of "practice makes perfect" might be the tip of an iceberg. Maybe there was friction between them that no one outside the family knew about. Now the boy's dead, Cluny's eaten up with remorse.'

'You could be right,' said Iris after a few moments' consideration. 'Saxe had plenty of talent, but he'd never have been the artist his father is . . . or used to be.' She sighed and ran her fingers through her bushy, mouse-brown hair. 'Don't suppose we'll ever know.'

Melissa got up to fill the kettle for coffee. 'By the way,' she said, 'you've hardly told me anything about your latest French trip. Did you do much painting? Did you visit *Les Châtaigniers*?' A couple of summers ago, Iris had tutored an art course in a remote village in the Cévennes where a friend of hers ran a study centre, and Melissa had gone with her to research a book. The region had impressed them with its beauty and grandeur; it was there that Iris had met Jack Hammond, with whom she had developed a relationship which was still quietly flourishing.

Melissa plugged in the kettle and reached for the coffee jar as she waited for a response to her questions, but none came. She glanced up to see Iris staring through the kitchen window, frowning. 'Something wrong?' she asked.

Iris started slightly, as if emerging from a reverie. 'No, nothing . . . just thinking. You were asking about France; it was okay.' She looked at her watch. 'I think if you don't mind I'll get back to the garden. Want to get as much done as I can; there's more rain on the way. Thanks for lunch, see you tomorrow.'

And she was gone, leaving Melissa to drink coffee on her own and to wonder, with some unease, what it was that Iris had on her mind. It wasn't the first time since her return from France that she had seemed evasive.

The village of Carston was tucked away in a fold of the Cotswold Hills about eight miles from Upper Benbury. The Manor lay hidden behind a stand of tall trees – no doubt planted long ago by a previous owner as a protection against northerly winds – and was surrounded by a high stone wall. The house was approached through wrought-iron gates and along a winding drive that sloped gently downwards until, in a final sweeping curve, it ended in a broad, gravelled area outside the main entrance.

Melissa parked the Golf in front of a low stone parapet overlooking the garden and for a few moments she and Iris sat admiring the prospect. To their right, a stream bubbled from a culvert and went tumbling downhill, frothing and sparkling over a miniature waterfall into a series of rocky pools before flowing away along the bottom of the valley. Ahead, the parapet was pierced by a shallow flight of steps leading to an informal arrangement of lawns dotted with ornamental trees and shrubs, rockeries bright with spring flowers, and borders and rosebeds promising a profusion of summer scent and colour. Everything bore the hallmark of an expert and dedicated gardener.

'What a magical spot!' exclaimed Melissa in delight.

'Lovely,' agreed Iris as they got out of the car. 'So's the house. Just look at it!' Her eyes shone as she recited its features. 'Genuine Cotswold tiled roof, six gables, umpteen ornamental chimneys, mullioned windows, stone porch . . . just asking to be put on canvas.'

'Let's hope Mrs G-N sees it that way.'

Iris shrugged philosophically. 'Can but try.'

'The boyfriend must have left her a packet,' observed Melissa as they approached the massive oak front door. 'A place like this costs the earth to keep up, and it's all immaculate.' She pressed the polished brass bell-push and a few seconds later they were admitted by a pleasant-faced woman who ushered them into a small, cosily furnished room where a cheerful fire burned on a stone hearth.

'Mrs Grantley-Newcombe will be with you in a moment,' she told them, and disappeared.

While they were waiting, they glanced round the room. Shelves on either side of the chimney-breast held books and an assortment of ornaments. On an occasional table were a number of photographs in silver frames and over the fireplace hung a painting of an imposing, colonial-style house in what was plainly a tropical setting. Melissa strolled over to examine the books; they were for the most part good quality editions of literary classics and appeared brand-new. Iris picked up a carved wooden toucan, scrutinised it with close interest, replaced it and went to study the picture.

'Somewhere in the Caribbean, I guess,' she commented.

'Jamaica, actually,' said a voice behind them. They

turned to see a petite, exquisitely-groomed woman of about forty-five who had just entered the room. With straight, glossy brown hair framing finely-chiselled features, she was still beautiful; as a girl, she must have been stunning. She came forward, glancing from one to the other with large blue eyes. 'I'm Dorinda Grantley-Newcombe. Which of you is Mrs Craig?'

'I am, but do please call me Melissa. This is my friend Iris Ash, who's very kindly come to help us.'

'I'm *reelly reelly* grateful to you both. Do call me Dorrie,' said their hostess, shaking each of them by the hand. 'You were admiring the picture,' she went on, looking up at it with a pleased smile. 'It's ever so old – it's been in my family for generations. That's my ancestral home near Kingston. My great-great-grandfather built it; he was a wealthy sugar plantation owner. Several generations of my family lived out there.'

Iris acknowledged the information with a brief nod.

'What brought you back to England?' she asked.

'My parents both died of a fever when I was ten and I was sent to boarding school in England. During the holidays, I lived with an aunt in London – when we were in this country, that is. We travelled abroad a lot, mostly on the continent.' Dorrie had evidently told her story many times; she spoke the words almost mechanically, like a child repeating a lesson, with little or no expression.

'Losing your parents must have been a pretty traumatic experience for you,' said Melissa sympathetically.

'Quite a change of climate too,' commented Iris, still studying the picture.

'I beg your pardon?'

'Lot colder in England than Jamaica.'

'Oh . . . yes, of course. But I was only a child, you see . . . one forgets so easily.' With heavily jewelled fingers, Dorrie fiddled with the gold chain at her throat. For a moment she appeared disconcerted, but quickly recovered her composure and said, 'Would you care for some coffee?'

'Shall we bring the things indoors first?' suggested Melissa.

'Good idea, Mel.' Iris was peering out of the window. 'Clouding over – looks like rain.'

'Oh, my staff will see to that.' Dorrie tugged at a bell-pull and a minute later the woman who had opened the front door entered. 'Bring the coffee please, Florence, and then get Tony to help you unload Mrs Craig's car and take all the things into the morning room.' She turned to her visitors. 'The decorators have only just finished in there so I'm not using it yet. There's plenty of space to spread everything out.'

'I understand the sale is being held here at the Manor,' said Melissa. 'It's a lovely setting.'

'That's right. We'll be using the stables and outbuildings as well, of course, for teas and a produce stall and so forth. Lady Sugden and Mrs Bridgton are organising all that – they're ever so nice, *real* ladies if you know what I mean, not like some I might mention.' Dorrie bunched her mouth into an 'I-could-say-a-lot-more-if-I-chose-to' expression.

'What about parking?' Melissa said quickly, anxious to avoid a discussion about personalities.

'In the paddock. Tony – Florence's husband – is organising that. Ah, thank you,' she went on as the housekeeper came in, put down a tray and withdrew. 'By the way,' she looked questioningly at Melissa, 'I heard Iris call you "Mel" – you aren't by any chance Mel Craig, the crime writer?'

'That's right.'

Dorrie's eyes shone. 'How exciting!' she exclaimed. 'I'm a great fan of yours, I read all your books and I think they're ever so clever.'

Melissa smiled as she accepted a cup of coffee. 'That's very kind. I'm glad you enjoy them.'

'I think all writers must be ever so clever,' said Dorrie. She turned to Iris. 'Are you a writer too?'

'No, I paint pictures and design wallpaper.'

Dorrie expressed more breathless admiration and it was not long before Iris managed to steer her round to the possibility of commissioning a painting of the manor, a suggestion which was embraced with enthusiasm. The discussion then turned to the matter in hand; by the time the task of sorting and pricing was finished and various organisational details, including the hiring of racks on which to display the clothes, had been settled, it was gone one o'clock.

'I feel dreadful at not inviting you to stay for lunch,' Dorrie apologised as she saw them to the door, 'but I have an appointment with my solicitor in less than an hour. Ah, here's Tony bringing the car round for me now.' A dark green Jaguar appeared round the angle of the house as she spoke and drew up in front of them.

'No problem. Glad to help, see you again soon,' said Iris.

Dorrie turned to Melissa. 'I'll give you a ring when I've organised the racks.'

'Oh, er, yes, of course,' said Melissa, her eyes on the Jaguar.

'I see you're admiring my car,' Dorrie purred. Her

expression reminded Melissa of a self-satisfied kitten. 'Tony looks after it like a baby.'

'It shows,' said Melissa with a smile.

The visitors took their leave. Neither spoke until they drove out of the gates and turned on to the main road. Then Iris said, 'She's a phoney.'

'She certainly is,' replied Melissa, surprised at hearing her own thoughts expressed aloud, 'but what makes *you* so sure?'

'The picture.'

'What about the picture?'

'Acrylic paint. In the style of the period . . . quite cleverly done . . . but the only antique thing about it is the frame.'

'I'd never have spotted that,' said Melissa admiringly. 'So what put you on to her?'

'The Jag. I recognised the number plate. If my guess is correct, Dorrie's real name is Daisy Grice, and she's no more descended from Jamaican sugar barons than you or I.'

'How d'you make that out?'

'It's quite a funny story. I'll tell you about it when we get home.'

Chapter Sixteen

Over a lunch of mushroom pâté and salad in Iris's kitchen, Melissa gave a racy description of her encounter with Laura Maddox in the multi-storey car park in Cheltenham, and of that lady's reaction to being ignored by the driver of a dark green Jaguar.

'I'm certain it was the same car because of the number plate,' she said, as she and Iris chuckled over the story. 'I only caught a glimpse of the driver's profile, but it was definitely a woman, a brunette . . . it must have been Dorrie. She couldn't get out of that car park quickly enough.'

'Understandable,' said Iris drily.

Melissa nodded. 'From what Laura Maddox was shouting at her, it sounded as if she'd either been a tom or else involved in something equally disreputable that she wouldn't want her county friends to hear about.'

'Dorrie talks like a Londoner. What about the Maddox woman?'

'She had a similar accent, but stronger. I think Dorrie's trying to hide hers, but she gives herself away every so often. I suppose that's what old Mother Bone-*ay* was sneering about.'

'I wonder . . .' Iris was looking thoughtful. 'Couldn't be certain, but . . .'

'But what?' prompted Melissa after a pause, during which Iris sat with knotted brows and half-closed eyes.

'Remember that model Cluny was on about?' she said at last. 'Couldn't remember her name, thought it began with a D?'

'The one you called a skinny little thing, and he insisted was a pocket Venus?'

'That's the one. Might have been Daisy. Dorrie's the right age, good bone structure, petite build . . .'

'You didn't recognise her, though?'

'It was thirty odd years ago,' Iris pointed out. 'Can't be sure. More salad?' She pushed the bowl across the table.

'Even supposing you're right, it's nothing to be ashamed of,' said Melissa, helping herself to tomatoes garnished with herbs from Iris's garden. 'Lots of young people do it to earn pocket money if they've got the looks.'

'True.'

'So maybe Daisy graduated to something more lucrative.'

'But less respectable.'

'Hardly surprising in a way,' Melissa concluded. 'With no father and a drug addict for a mother . . .'

'Wonder how she got mixed up with Maddox?' observed Iris after a pause.

Melissa frowned, trying to recall more of the flood of gratuitous information that had been hurled at her. 'She was screaming something about her – that is, Laura's – father giving Daisy a job, and how it was through them that she'd met a rich boyfriend.'

'So maybe father was a pimp.'

Melissa pulled a face at mention of the disgusting trade.

'It could tie in with what Gloria told me about how Dorrie got her money.'

'Let's hope for her sake the Maddox doesn't track her down. Wonder why the phoney Jamaican family?' Plainly intrigued, Iris sat back and began absently fiddling with the tortoiseshell slides that kept her springy hair in some sort of order. 'And why come to the Cotswolds?'

'That's something we'll probably never know. Life seems to be full of unsolved mysteries at the moment.'

'Some more serious than others.' Iris's expression became grim. 'Still no news about the Smiler, I take it? Or Natalie?'

Melissa shook her head. 'I'm seeing Ken tomorrow evening. He may be able to tell me something.'

In the event, the position turned out to be exactly the opposite.

The fine weather looked set to last for the weekend and on Saturday morning Melissa got up early, put on jeans and a sweater and was in her garden by nine o'clock. Presently Iris, who had already announced her intention to visit an art exhibition in Oxford and then go on to spend the night with friends, called over the fence with a reminder about feeding Binkie before driving off in her vintage Morris.

Her departure left Melissa with a sense of desolation. She had more or less recovered from the shock of finding Martha's corpse and her common sense assured her that she was unlikely to be targeted by the Smiler. Nevertheless, the realisation that she was alone in her cottage, with no human being other than the occasional party of ramblers within earshot, caused uneasy twinges in her stomach. Then she remembered with relief that Ken was coming that evening. If he wanted to stay for the night

– which he almost certainly would – well, maybe, even though he would read it as yet another step on the road to a permanent commitment . . . to her surprise, Melissa found herself humming a tune as she toiled away in her vegetable patch.

At eleven o'clock she went indoors and made a cup of coffee. She stood at the kitchen window while drinking it, looking out with satisfaction at the neat rows of vigorously sprouting broad beans and onions, separated by strips of dark, freshly hoed earth. Bordering the little plot was a hawthorn hedge, its tightly woven network of thorny branches a haven for nesting birds. Beyond lay the sheltered, peaceful valley through which she and Iris often walked and which she had come to love so well. In the space of a few years, she had put down roots here, become part of a way of life whose rhythms matched the turn of the seasons. The thought of leaving it was like a physical pain.

Her reverie was broken by the sound of the telephone. Genty Donovan was on the line. She sounded tense, almost nervous.

'Melissa, I've had the strangest telephone call . . . from a Doctor Anderson. Natalie has been transferred to a psychiatric unit and she's asking to see me.'

'That's interesting. Did the doctor say why?'

'Not really, except that she seems to think it's a step forward. Up till now, Natalie's hardly said a word about why she took the tablets . . . or about anything else.'

'It sounds as if there's been a breakthrough. When are you going?'

'Doctor Anderson asked if I'd go as soon as possible, before Natalie changes her mind.' There was a pause before Genty continued hesitantly, 'I was wondering if you could give me a lift, if you're not busy. My car's having a new clutch fitted and Sirry's using hers this morning to take Father shopping.'

'Of course. I'm grubby from the garden – give me a few minutes to clean up and change and I'll be right with you.'

'I'm awfully grateful.'

'No problem.'

Genty said very little during the drive to the clinic. The hint of tension that Melissa had detected over the telephone was still apparent, although plainly she was trying to keep it under control. She sat grasping the strap of her seat belt, occasionally tugging at it with jerky movements that seemed to indicate suppressed emotion or excitement.

'I wonder if you'll be allowed to see Natalie alone, or if there'll be a police officer present,' Melissa said casually as she turned through the entrance to the clinic.

Genty started, as if her thoughts had been far away. 'I've no idea,' she said absently.

It occurred to Melissa that she might not be looking forward to the interview. 'Would you like me to come in with you?' she offered. 'If they'll let me, that is.'

Genty appeared surprised at the suggestion. 'I don't want to sound rude, but I don't think Natalie would talk in front of a stranger.'

'You're probably right. I just thought you seemed a tad edgy.'

'Edgy?' Genty sounded almost offended. 'Why should I be?'

'I don't know. I'm sorry – forget it. Anyway, here we

are.' Melissa pulled up by the front door. 'You go on in while I park the car.'

'How will I know where to find you?'

'Don't worry – I'll make contact.'

Genty got out without further comment and disappeared into the building, while Melissa headed for the car park. It was already fairly full and it took her several minutes to find a vacant space. As she backed into it and switched off the engine, she noticed a young woman in nurse's uniform emerge from a side door and head in her direction. There was something familiar about her; when she drew closer, Melissa recognised her as one of the girls who had been sitting with Natalie in Thanebury church during the memorial service . . . and who had hustled her away before she had a chance to talk to Genty. Well, there was nothing to prevent the two from meeting now.

The nurse seemed in a hurry. Thinking that she might have news of Natalie's progress, Melissa was on the point of going to intercept her when she saw her stop beside a car parked a short distance away, open the passenger door and get in. The engine was already running; as the car moved off, Melissa recognised the driver as being another of the so-called 'Daughters of Light'. She noticed something else. Passing within a few feet of her, yet obviously unaware of her presence, the two girls were exchanging satisfied glances and gestures of triumph.

Melissa became uneasy; the body language that she had witnessed was not indicative of relief at the progress of a sick friend, but of delight in a mission accomplished. As soon as the car was out of sight, she hurried back to the main entrance and went to the reception desk. A middle-aged woman with a stolid expression raised her eyes from a register that lay open before her and said, 'Yes?'

'I've come to see a patient called Natalie; can you direct me to her room, please?' said Melissa.

The woman's face seemed to close up. 'Natalie who?' she asked coldly.

'I don't know her surname, I'm afraid. She's a patient of Doctor Anderson and she's just been transferred here from Stowbridge General Hospital . . . my friend Miss Donovan has come to visit her and I'd like to see her as well.'

'I know the patient you're speaking of, and no unauthorised visitors are allowed access to her.' The woman spoke with a slow deliberation and a touch of officiousness that set Melissa's hackles rising.

'So how do I get authorisation?' she asked.

'I suggest you telephone Doctor Anderson's secretary on Monday to make an appointment.' The receptionist turned a page in her register in what was obviously intended as a gesture of dismissal.

'I'm afraid it can't wait till Monday,' Melissa protested. 'It's very important that I see her right away!'

'I'm sorry, I can't make any exceptions. If you wish to leave a message, I will see that Doctor Anderson gets it.'

Melissa drew a deep breath and tried a different approach. 'I'd like to speak to whoever is in charge here,' she said, keeping her voice even with an effort.

An angry flush spread over the woman's heavy features. 'I have authority to refuse admission,' she said stiffly, 'and for the last time . . .'

'Having a spot of bother, Mrs Craig?' said an urbane voice.

Melissa swung round and met the slightly supercilious gaze of Acting Chief Inspector Desmond Holloway.

Forgetting her dislike of the man in her relief at his timely arrival, she said, 'Inspector, I'd like a private word with you . . . about Natalie.'

'Certainly. Come with me – I'm just going up to see her. It's all right, I'll vouch for Mrs Craig,' he informed the receptionist, who had evidently recognised him, but was looking distinctly annoyed at being overruled.

Holloway led the way up a flight of carpeted stairs and along a corridor. Seated outside a door at the far end was a young woman police constable, who stood up as they approached.

'Everything okay, Mandy?'

'Yes sir. Ms Donovan and Doctor Anderson have just gone in to see Natalie.'

'Good.' Holloway turned to Melissa. 'Now, what's the problem?'

'I saw a young woman in nurse's uniform leaving the clinic about five minutes ago. I recognised her . . . she was with Natalie in church on the day of the memorial service.'

'I see.' Holloway showed no reaction. 'Is that all?'

'No. There was a car waiting for her, driven by another of the girls who were with Natalie that evening. They looked excited and gave one another the thumbs up, as though they'd achieved something special. Then they drove away in a great hurry.' Suddenly, Melissa remembered something else. 'I have reason to believe that girl isn't really a nurse . . . I'm sure Mrs Aggs said that all the "Daughters of Light" were college students.'

Holloway's expression altered at the final words. 'You're saying the girls you saw are members of that hot-gospeller's fan club?' he said sharply. 'Are you sure?'

'Absolutely.'

'And one of them's been here?' Holloway rounded on the young WPC. 'Mandy, has anyone at all been in to see Natalie within the past half-hour?'

'Only a nurse, to take her pulse and temperature,' said Mandy nervously.

'Did you stay in the room with her?'

'I . . .' The girl blushed and looked uncomfortable. 'Actually, Sir, I was . . . well . . . I needed the loo quite badly . . . I asked the nurse to be sure and stay with Natalie until I got back.'

'And did she?'

'Oh yes . . . I was only gone a few minutes . . . and then she went away.'

The look that Holloway turned on the young officer was enough, as Melissa put it later when describing the day's events to Ken Harris, to set fire to an igloo. 'I'll speak to you later,' he snapped as he grabbed the handle of the door. He turned to Melissa. 'You'd better come in too,' he said.

There were three people in the room. Natalie, fully dressed, was sitting in an armchair with Genty in a second chair opposite her. A woman in a white coat was standing between them. They turned with startled faces as Holloway marched in with Melissa at his heels.

'Forgive the intrusion, Doctor Anderson,' he said brusquely. 'Something's cropped up.'

The doctor, a youngish woman with pointed features and dark, shingled hair, glared at him through heavy tortoiseshell glasses attached to a cord round her neck.

'Really, Inspector, this kind of interruption is very unsettling for my patient,' she said impatiently. 'Can't it wait?'

'No, I'm afraid it can't,' he replied. Making a visible effort to soften his manner, he added, 'Perhaps we could have a word outside?'

The doctor hesitated, then said, 'Very well.' She turned to Natalie. 'You'll be all right with Ms Donovan, won't you dear? I'll only be a minute.'

Natalie nodded without speaking, her head lowered. She was a pale girl, on the plump side, with a wary, defensive air that reminded Melissa of a cornered animal.

Doctor Anderson ushered the intruders outside and closed the door behind her. 'You have come at a most unfortunate moment, Inspector,' she said severely. 'For the first time since her admission to this clinic, Natalie has showed signs of being ready to talk to us.'

Holloway ignored the reproof. He turned to Melissa and said, 'Tell the doctor what you saw.'

Briefly, Melissa described the incident in the car park. 'I became uneasy because I remembered how anxious those girls were to prevent Miss Donovan from speaking to Natalie in church,' she added.

Doctor Anderson frowned and compressed her lips. 'It's very strange,' she muttered. 'This morning, Natalie suddenly asked to see Ms Donovan, but when she arrived, she hardly said a word except "Hello".'

'It sounds as if there's a connection,' said Holloway. 'I think I'd better have a word with those young ladies. Meanwhile, Doctor, you see what you can coax out of Natalie.'

'If I think it appropriate,' the doctor said stiffly. 'This is very unfortunate,' she repeated, 'but we must persevere with the treatment so, if you'll excuse me, I'll go back to my patient.'

Melissa put out a hand to detain her. 'Just a moment,

Doctor,' she said urgently. 'Would you ask Natalie if that girl gave her anything?'

'You think she might have done?'

'I can't be sure, but if she did, Natalie has probably hidden it.'

'Hidden what?'

'I don't know.' Melissa was becoming flustered; the possibility that had just occurred to her was so fantastic that she could not bring herself to put it into words for fear of attracting scorn – either from the doctor, who appeared unconvinced, or from Holloway, who looked anything but pleased at her intervention. Yet the scenario that was building up in her head was too chilling, too frightening to ignore.

'Please, Doctor Anderson, see what you can find out,' she begged. 'It could be terribly important.'

'Wait here.' The doctor re-entered the room, closing the door firmly behind her. Through it, her voice could be heard rising and falling, pleading and cajoling, but although the listeners outside strained their ears they only caught the occasional word. Nothing further happened for several minutes; then there was a high-pitched scream, followed by a burst of hysterical crying. The next moment, Genty came out of the room. The others caught a glimpse of Natalie sobbing in the doctor's arms before the door closed again.

Genty gave Holloway a transparent plastic sachet containing what appeared to be individually wrapped confectionery. 'Doctor Anderson doesn't know yet what the bogus nurse said to Natalie,' she told him, 'but she found this hidden in the bed.'

Holloway took the bag and examined it carefully. 'It's still sealed,' he commented and turned it over.

'Chocolate marzipan *dragées*,' he said, reading from the label. 'Nothing sinister there. Probably the girl's favourite. Let her have them back.' He handed the sachet to Genty and turned a patronising look on Melissa. 'Satisfied?' he asked.

'Did you say marzipan?' Genty stared at the bag of confectionery in her hand with eyes that had widened in alarm.

'That's right. What about it?'

'Natalie has a fatal allergy to anything containing almonds. It would take only one of these to kill her. It's true,' she insisted on seeing Holloway's sceptical expression. 'She nearly died once when she was a toddler through putting a piece of marzipan off a Christmas cake in her mouth.'

'How do you know this?' he demanded.

'It came out once during a class on Titian and how Lucrezia Borgia was one of his patrons . . . and someone mentioned poisons . . . and Natalie said half jokingly that if ever anyone wanted to murder her . . .' Genty's voice trembled as the significance of what she was saying began to sink in. 'Inspector, do you suppose that girl knew, and deliberately gave Natalie . . . but why?'

'That's what I intend to find out.' Holloway retrieved the sachet, put it in his pocket and then rounded on the WPC who was still seated by the door. 'Mandy! Turn that room over, make sure there's nothing else stashed away that shouldn't be there.'

Mandy leapt to her feet. 'Sir!' she said, and reached for the door handle.

'And from now on,' Holloway continued, 'don't you *ever* leave that girl alone for a second with anyone except a police colleague or the doctor. Understand?'

'Yes, sir,' quavered Mandy.

'Not ever,' he repeated, 'even if it means peeing in your pants!'

As Mandy scuttled into Natalie's room, Melissa caught Holloway's eye where, for a split second, she detected the ghost of a twinkle. Perhaps the man was human after all.

'I suppose we might as well go home,' said Genty, as the door closed in their faces and Holloway went haring off down the corridor, leaving them on their own.

'I guess so.'

When they were back on the road to Upper Benbury, Genty said, 'What gave you the idea those girls might want to harm Natalie?'

'I don't know . . . a hunch, I suppose.' Even now, Melissa could not bring herself to voice what might be totally irrational fears. In any case, she had yet to think things through systematically. 'By the way,' she added, 'there were at least three of them in church with Natalie. Were any of them present when she was talking about her allergy to almonds?'

'No, they're all on different courses. They don't attend any of my classes.'

'So they might not even know about it.' Melissa heaved a sigh. 'Oh dear, perhaps I've sent Inspector Holloway on a fool's errand. He won't be best pleased with me.'

Genty chuckled. She seemed more relaxed than she had been earlier. 'I wouldn't let it worry you,' she said.

They arrived back at Larkfield Barn to find Cluny and his elder daughter unloading their shopping. They looked up and waved as Melissa drove into the yard. Sirry, a bulging brown paper carrier clasped in her arms, came across to enquire how the visit had gone.

'A bit inconclusive in a way . . . Genty will tell you about it,' said Melissa. Her eye fell on a bottle of champagne protruding from the carrier. 'Whose birthday is it?' she asked.

Sirry looked at first startled and then slightly embarrassed as she followed Melissa's glance. 'Oh, er, no one's. We just thought we'd treat ourselves. That's right, isn't it Genty?' She glanced at her sister for confirmation.

'Of course dear.' The two women exchanged one of their almost childlike smiles.

'Me daughters are telling me things are going to get better from now on and it's to the future we have to be looking,' said Cluny, who had wandered over to join them. There was a noticeable change in him; his eyes had lost their emptiness and there was a spontaneity in his manner that she had never seen before. Was he at last coming out of his private hell? If so, it had to be partly through Iris's influence. She would be delighted at the news.

'They're quite right, and it's great to see you looking so much better,' said Melissa warmly. 'Enjoy your celebration.'

That evening, Melissa confided her suspicions to Ken Harris. To her relief, he took them seriously. 'At least the people looking after Natalie will be on their guard now,' he said. 'If that was a deliberate attempt on the part of those girls to harm her, they won't get another chance.' With knotted brows, he stared moodily out of the window. Melissa had a shrewd idea that he was feeling a certain frustration at not being actively involved in the case, and his next words confirmed it. 'Wish I could be a fly on the wall during the interviews,' he muttered, half to himself.

'Matt will keep you in touch with developments,' she said and, by way of a change of subject, added, 'Did your latest case turn out well?'

'I think so. The client seems satisfied . . . and she's going to recommend me to one of her business friends.'

'I didn't know you've been working for a woman. Is she very high-powered?'

'As a racing car, and glamorous to boot,' he said with a sly grin. 'Still, you'll make an acceptable substitute.' He reached out and pulled her into an embrace that she had neither the strength nor the inclination to resist. 'Any idea where you'd like to eat?' he asked after an interval.

'They said on the radio at six o'clock that there might be snow over the Cotswolds tonight,' she said in her most matter-of-fact tone, 'so I've laid on a couple of steaks and a bottle of wine. We don't want to get stuck in a snowdrift, do we?'

'Absolutely not,' he agreed.

Chapter Seventeen

There was no mention of the Thanebury case in the Sunday papers that Melissa collected from the village shop. Ken Harris called Matt Waters at his home, only to learn that he had been off duty with a feverish cold since Friday and knew even less than they did. He did, however, promise to see what he could find out. At mid-day, a brief item on the radio news announced that several people were being questioned in connection with the deaths and that a further statement would be issued 'in the near future'.

Harris made several more attempts to contact Matt during the morning, but each time the line was engaged. After lunch, he and Melissa set off for a walk along the valley. The threatened snow had been little more than a light powdering, insufficient to cause serious inconvenience but enough to turn the landscape into a sparkling fairyland before vanishing in the early spring sunshine. They returned to Hawthorn Cottage refreshed, invigorated . . . and still burning with curiosity. A further call to Matt Waters' number produced a ringing tone, but no reply.

'I wonder if Bertha Aggs knows anything,' Melissa remarked, as Ken impatiently slammed down the phone. 'I think I'll give her a bell.'

'Good idea. Be careful what you say, though.'

'Don't worry, I won't let on I know anything except what's been on the radio.'

To her surprise, a man's voice answered the telephone. When Bertha came on the line, she exclaimed, 'Oh Melissa, I'm so glad you called. Such wonderful news!' Her voice dropped as she added, 'That was Raymond, he's come back to me. We're really going to work at our marriage.'

'I'm delighted to hear it,' said Melissa sincerely. 'Tell me, Bertha, have you heard the news? Do you know who's been arrested?'

'Oh, Melissa, it's absolutely dreadful. Everyone in the village is so shocked. A retired clergyman from Stowbridge came to take the service this morning and he told us Mr Jarman and three of the young women he calls his "Daughters of Light" were helping the police with their enquiries. We were all stunned. Melissa, do you really believe they had anything to do with those terrible murders?'

'It begins to look like it. We'll have to wait for further news. Bertha, I'm so happy that your own problems have been sorted out . . . take care.'

'I will. And once again, thank you for everything.'

'You're welcome.' Melissa put the phone down and reported the conversation. 'I guess that's one of our mysteries solved, although I imagine it'll be ages before we know the full story.'

'One of them?' For a moment Harris looked puzzled, then said, 'I suppose you're thinking of Martha Willis?'

'Among other things, although I imagine she'll turn out to be another of Gareth Jarman's victims. Come to think of it, it does seem fishy, the way he came charging over here, supposedly offering comfort and support. I wonder how he came to hear about her . . . and why he decided she was ready for eternal bliss.'

'If it *was* him – I'm still not convinced that we aren't dealing with a very nasty copycat killer,' said Harris thoughtfully, 'although I understand the Super and Des Holloway are beginning to have doubts about that theory.'

'Because of the smile?' The memory of the painted rictus still had the power to cause a spasm in Melissa's vitals.

'Right. Except for the difference in the lipstick used, it was a carbon copy of the other killings. Just the same, I have this gut feeling . . .' He broke off, leaving the remark in the air.

'I hope you're mistaken, that's all.' Once again, the memory of the nightmare scene in Martha Willis's bedroom came surging back. 'Because if you're not . . .'

He put an arm round her shoulders and she leaned against him, drawing comfort from the contact with his substantial frame. 'Darling, if you're seriously worried, you can always move into my place for a while,' he said. 'I have to be away at odd times, so I can't be here with you every night.'

'That's sweet of you, but I couldn't leave Iris on her own. Not that either of us is seriously scared of being attacked,' she added, willing it to be true. 'It's talking about it that gives me the willies.'

'Okay, we'll talk about something else. You hinted at other mysteries. Are they real ones, or part of Nathan Latimer's latest case?'

Melissa pulled a face. 'Nathan hasn't got a case at the moment. I was thinking of Daisy Grice, alias Dorinda

Grantley-Newcombe.' She described the visit she and Iris had paid to Carston Manor and their subsequent speculation concerning the true background of its present owner, ending with a graphic account of Laura Maddox doing a furious war dance after the retreating Jaguar. Instead of the expected chuckle, however, the story was received with a frown.

'Is this the same woman you saw with young Clifford Fenn?' Harris asked. Melissa nodded. 'You're sure?' he insisted.

'Of course I'm sure. Do you know anything about her?'

'Only what you told me before. I passed that on to Matt Waters, but I haven't heard anything further. From what you've just said, she's an even less desirable associate for a police officer than we thought.'

'Maybe he's doing some undercover work. Or under-the-covers work,' she added flippantly, but still he did not smile.

'You mentioned that this Laura Maddox and the other woman – Dorrie, you called her – sound like Londoners?' he said.

'Home Counties, anyway. What are you up to now?' she demanded as he went to fetch his jacket and rummaged in the inside pocket. He brought out an address book and began thumbing through the pages.

'Mind if I call London?' he said.

Recognising the purposeful gleam in his eye, she knew it was pointless to ask more questions at this stage. 'Help yourself. Use the phone in the study if you like. I'll go and make some tea.'

He was gone for several minutes. When he came downstairs he joined Melissa in the kitchen and sat watching her while she poured tea and cut slices of fruit cake, his expression thoughtful.

'Are you going to tell me what all this is about?' she asked.

'I thought the name Maddox rang a bell,' he said, 'so I called an ex-colleague who transferred to London and asked if it meant anything to him.'

'And?' she prompted impatiently as he stopped talking to tackle a slice of cake.

'It may not be the same family, of course, but Frank says a Trevor Maddox was sent down a few years ago for procuring. I remember the case now; there was quite a bit of scandal as some of the clients were public figures and the tabloids had a field day. There was a daughter as well, but he couldn't recall her name. They tried to get her for conspiracy, but the case against her had to be dropped for lack of evidence.'

'Hmm. As you say, not the kind of company an up-and-coming young copper should keep,' Melissa commented, 'but why are you so concerned?'

He gave a rueful smile and held out his teacup to be refilled. 'As you may have noticed, once a detective, always a detective,' he admitted. 'Besides, if young Fenn really is making a fool of himself over this old tart, he should at least know what kind of woman she is. How about some more cake?'

'Help yourself,' said Melissa absently. Her mind had switched back to the scene between Laura Maddox and Clifford Fenn and the final exchange of remarks between them. '*When will I see you again?*' '*Not till you've done what I asked you, sweetie pie.*' '*But it could be days before I get the chance to . . .*' The chance to do what?

'Penny for 'em?'

Melissa put down her empty cup and began fiddling with the cake knife. 'Ken, there's something I didn't tell you about Laura Maddox and Clifford Fenn.' She repeated the scraps of conversation she had overheard. 'There was nothing to suggest that what she wanted him to do was dodgy, or had anything to do with his job,' she protested, seeing his look of disapproval.

'That's true. Still, I think I'll mention it to Matt, if I can get hold of him.' He reached for the telephone on the wall beside him and tapped out the number; this time he got through. After a brief conversation he hung up and said, 'Matt will be back at work tomorrow and he'll pass the information on.'

'Has he been able to find out any more about the people being questioned?'

'Only to confirm what Bertha Aggs told you. Jarman and three of his handmaidens were picked up yesterday evening and they're still being interviewed at two separate stations.' His manner suddenly altered; he gave a satisfied grin and rubbed his hands together with undisguised relish. 'This is going to be interesting!'

'Kenneth Harris, when are you going to get it through your head that you're no longer a policeman?' said Melissa despairingly.

'Just keeping my hand in. You never know.' He glanced at his watch. 'I must be getting home. I've got a surveillance job tomorrow and I want to be in position before it gets light.'

Monday morning's news bulletin contained the surprising news that the man being questioned in connection with the Thanebury murders had been released without charge. Three other people were still being held and an extension had been applied for and granted. The evening brought no further official statement, but a brief call from Ken Harris set Melissa's curiosity spiralling out of control.

'The media will go wild over this one when it gets out,' he said. 'I've picked up some details, but it's totally off the record and I've been threatened with loss of potency if I breathe a word to a living soul.'

'Oh Ken, surely you can tell me,' she begged. 'You know I won't . . .'

'Sorry. Got to go now.' And he rang off.

It was not until Tuesday that the mid-day news carried the dramatic announcement that three young women had been formally charged with the murder of Emily Twigg on or about the seventh of January, while a fourth had been charged with conspiracy to pervert the course of justice. All had been remanded – three in custody – for psychiatric reports and it was likely that further charges would follow.

'Ken, what on earth does it mean?' Melissa demanded when he came to Hawthorn Cottage that evening. 'And don't give me any of that "my lips are sealed" stuff, or you won't get any supper!' she threatened. 'My kitchen isn't bugged and I promise I won't be calling the *Sun* the minute you go home.'

'One thing's for sure, and that is that the shrinks are going to be busy for a while,' he told her. 'What's been coming out in the interviews is unbelievable. Those young witches had formed themselves into a kind of Murder Incorporated, specifically to dispose of old people whose quality of life they considered so poor that it was an act of mercy to do away with them. At least, that's what two of them are claiming. The third openly admitted that she was doing it for society as a whole, so that the "resources" they were supposedly using up could be diverted to something or someone more worth while. The mind boggles – I've come across some nasty cases in my time, but my blood runs cold just thinking about this one. Give me a scotch, there's a love.'

'You know where it is so help yourself – and I think I'll join you,' said Melissa. She too was experiencing a sick wave of horror as the appalling truth sank in. 'So all the time these so-called "Daughters of Light" were running in and out of these poor old people's houses, pretending to do good works, they were planning to kill them. It doesn't bear thinking about!'

'"Daughters of Light" my foot! "Handmaidens from Hell" would be a better description. They're psychotic, of course, barking bloody mad, but they'll probably get away with manslaughter on the grounds of diminished responsibility.' He stared morosely into his whisky glass. 'Dear God, what a world we live in!' he muttered.

'I reckon it's Jarman's responsibility as well, winding them up with all that talk of eternal bliss,' asserted Melissa. She tipped some rice into boiling water, stirred it, covered the pan with a lid and sat down with the drink Ken had poured for her. 'He should have realised that there was something more than just teenage crushes involved – the fanaticism in the way those young harpies looked at him was spine-chilling.' She shuddered at the memory.

'I gather he's devastated at the interpretation they've been putting on his words.'

'So he should be. Did they kill Martha too?'

'I understand one of them claims they did, but the others deny it. It'll take time to piece the complete truth together. There's a hell of a long way to go before the case gets to court.'

'What about Natalie? I take it she's the one facing the lesser charges?'

'Right. It seems that she's been so much under the influence of the others – and so terrified of them – that she was scared to open her mouth. Once she was assured that they had all been detained and couldn't get at her, she began to talk. It'll take time to get the full story out of her, but the gist of it seems to be that she had some idea of what they were up to, but didn't dare say anything. It wasn't part of their plan that she should find any of the bodies, and when she did, and went into shock, they got worried in case she blurted out something to incriminate them.'

'So that's why they wouldn't let her talk to Genty in church that evening,' said Melissa thoughtfully. 'But they couldn't be behind her all the time. They must have known she saw Genty at college and . . .'

'Exactly.' Ken's expression grew even grimmer. 'Now we come to the really fiendish twist. It's almost certain that it was because of the pressure they put on her that she tried to kill herself. She was as much swayed by them as they were by Jarman, so she swallowed a load of paracetomol tablets rather than betray them. Fortunately, her mother found her and the medics managed to pump it out of her before it did irreversible damage.'

'And once she was in the care of experts who would be sure to get the truth from her sooner or later, her so-called friends . . .' Melissa broke off and made a helpless gesture, unable to find words to express her revulsion at the evil that had been done.

'You've got it,' Ken muttered. Despite many years of police work and first-hand experience of the depths to which the human animal can sink, he was plainly affected by the calculating manner in which three apparently civilised young women had persecuted a fellow creature. 'They were determined that nothing should interfere with what they saw as their sacred mission, and they soon hit on an alternative means of disposing of the threat.'

'The chocolate marzipan, of course!' exclaimed Melissa. 'So they did know about her allergy. She'd have died in agony . . . how unspeakably wicked!'

Ken put a hand over hers and squeezed it gently. 'Try not to dwell on it,' he said. 'Just be thankful the Super and his team got on to them before they had a chance to claim another victim.' His voice held a hint of teasing as he added, 'with invaluable assistance from Melissa Craig!'

She made a brave attempt at a smile. 'You do believe it's over, don't you?'

'I sincerely hope so.'

Chapter Eighteen

Thursday brought a telephone call from Joe Martin, Melissa's agent, just back from a trip to California.

'It sounds wonderful,' she said after listening to his accounts of visits to the Yosemite National Park, the Napa Valley vineyards and the many delights of San Francisco. 'I've never been to the West Coast.'

'You should have said so – you could have come with me. We'd have had a lot of fun.'

'Yes, well, I was too busy finishing a novel, wasn't I? I'm just another of your wage slaves, helping to pay for your exotic lifestyle.'

'Of course, I was forgetting. You do the work and I get the perks, haha! It so happens I stopped off in New York on my way home to see your American publisher. I've tied up a very nice deal for *Simply Dead.*'

'That's good. How nice?' He named a figure and she said warmly, 'That *is* nice. Thank you very much, Joe.'

'You see, I really do have your interests at heart – in more ways than one.'

'I know,' she said gently. The subtle change in his tone made her feel guilty. He had been quietly in love with her for a long time now; she had only to say the word and he would give her the moon. He was good-looking, charming and intelligent, and he led a lifestyle that she would no doubt have enjoyed sharing. So why did she have to fall for a slightly overweight and far from glamorous policeman turned private investigator who worked impossible hours? Relationships could be baffling at times.

'Mel, are you still there?' Joe's voice, a trifle impatient, brought her back to earth.

'I'm here. I didn't catch what you just said though.'

'I only asked how things were in your Cotswold hide-away. What's Nathan Latimer going to get up to next?'

'I'm sending him on a vacation . . . somewhere far away where I've never been so there won't be a case for him to work on.'

'That doesn't follow. Plenty of writers set books in places they don't know first-hand.'

'Not this writer.'

'So what's the big idea?'

'I want to have a chat with you some time about his future. I think his creator needs a change of direction. And in reply to your other question, things have been rather nasty here for the past couple of weeks.' In a few words, punctuated by exclamations of horror at the other end of the line, she outlined the grisly story. 'This morning's papers are full of it,' she finished. 'I'm surprised you didn't know.'

'I only got back to London last night and I haven't had time to read the papers. Mel, you must have had a fearful shock. Are you sure you're okay?'

'I'm fine. Everyone's been wonderful . . . especially Ken Harris. He's a tower of strength.'

'I'm glad to hear it.' Joe's voice went suddenly flat. 'Well, give me time to catch up with things at the office and I'll be in touch again. Good bye for now.'

Melissa frowned as she replaced the receiver. That had been a bit cruel . . . but it was time he faced up to the fact that, fond as she was of him, they would never be more than friends. Yet things could have been so different.

She was so lost in thought that when the telephone rang again, she jumped. She picked it up to find an agitated Dorrie Grantley-Newcombe on the line.

'Melissa, I hope you won't mind my bothering you, but something dreadful's happened and I don't know what to do or which way to turn . . . I thought you might be able to . . . I mean, I know I ought to go to the police, but I daren't, it will all come out and they'll think I . . .'

Melissa broke in as her caller became increasingly incoherent. 'Dorrie, do calm down and tell me what this is all about.'

'I . . . I can't tell you on the phone.' The voice sank to a quavering whisper. 'Melissa, are you very busy? Could you possibly come and . . . I do need someone to advise me . . . please.'

Melissa gave a resigned sigh. From her study window, she could see Iris already hard at work in her garden. There were still plenty of jobs to be done out there, the weather was fine, she had no other commitments . . . at least, there had been none until, out of the blue, had come this urgent plea from someone she hardly knew.

Over the line she could hear the unmistakable sounds of a woman in deep distress. It would have taken a heart of stone to turn her away.

'I'll be with you in half an hour,' she promised, and cut short Dorrie's stammered thanks by hanging up.

When she reached Carston Manor, Dorrie herself opened the front door. She appeared to have recovered her composure, but the brightness in her manner struck

Melissa as forced and fragile. 'I've sent Tony to Swindon to deliver some papers to my solicitor, and Florence wanted to do some shopping so I said she could go along too,' she explained as she led the way into the room where Melissa and Iris had been received on their first visit. 'That way, we can be certain no one will overhear us. Do sit down. Would you like some coffee?'

Remembering her near-hysterical performance on the telephone, Melissa suspected that she had steadied herself with something stronger than caffeine. She was as perfectly groomed as ever, but her hands were not entirely steady, there were lines about her mouth and shadows under her eyes that had not been there before, and the careful make-up could not hide the fact that she had been crying.

She poured coffee from an electric percolator saying, 'I hope it's to your liking. Do you take cream and sugar?' before handing over a bone china cup and saucer and then sitting down. There was a pause before she said hesitantly, 'This is the first time for ages that I've made my own coffee. I haven't always had servants to do it for me, you see – in fact, there was a time when I couldn't even afford to drink it.'

'Yes, I know,' said Melissa gently.

Dorrie shot her a look of mingled astonishment and alarm. 'You do? How?'

'Your real name is Daisy Grice, isn't it?'

Dorrie's eyes bulged and she jumped so violently that some of her coffee slopped into the saucer. 'Who told you?' she asked shakily. 'Was it Laura Maddox? Do you know her?'

'Not exactly, but I heard her shouting abuse after a retreating car a couple of weeks or so ago,' Melissa explained. 'I only caught a glimpse of the driver, but I remembered the number because it was so distinctive. As soon as I saw your car, I recognised it.'

'I see.' Dorrie knotted her brows, then suddenly put a manicured finger to her forehead to smooth out the lines. Even in her agitation her looks, once no doubt her chief – possibly her only – asset, were important to her. There was a hint of unease in her voice as she asked, 'Did Laura tell you anything about me?'

Melissa made a snap decision to be selective with the truth. 'Something about the two of you once being friends, but that you don't want to know her any more,' she said.

'That's more or less right,' Dorrie admitted, 'but . . .' Leaving the sentence unfinished, she stared down at her coffee but made no move to drink it.

'Don't you think it would be better if you were to tell me why you asked me to come here?' Melissa suggested after a long pause. *Although I can probably guess*, she added mentally. *Somehow, Laura has tracked you down and is trying a spot of blackmail. Pay up or your social standing among the county's smart set is on the line. But what the hell do you expect me to do about it?*

Dorrie put down her untouched coffee and began nervously interlacing and then separating her fingers.

'Laura was good to me at first,' she began. 'I'd run away from home and was living in a squat when she found me. I couldn't get work, except a few hours a week posing for art students, so I was pretty desperate. She said she could get me a job that paid good money. She took me home and introduced me to her Dad. He invited me to stay in their house, bought me a lot of expensive clothes, treated me like another daughter – he said that was how he thought of me – and after a while he asked me if I'd like to work for him. He explained that he was running an agency, providing escorts for businessmen. That side of it was legitimate, of course, but it wasn't long before he began introducing me to men who wanted more than just an escort. Maddox was a pimp with some very high-class clients.'

The sad little confession, which more than confirmed what Ken Harris had already discovered, moved inexorably on. After an initial reluctance, Daisy Grice had come to accept the situation; the clients were on the whole not unreasonable in their demands and the pay was generous. As a child, living in the squalid council flat where her mother spent most of her time in a drug-induced stupor, she had taken refuge in a dream world, a world full of the rich and famous among whom she ranked as an equal. She had quickly recognised that, in real life, some people were better-spoken and had better manners than others. She tried to copy them, in spite of the fact that her school friends – and even her mother, when she was rational – mocked and taunted her. Life under the aegis of Trevor Maddox might not have been quite the stuff of her dreams, but it was a vast improvement on what she had known earlier. And it brought her into contact with men of education and taste, who wined and dined her, took her on trips to Europe, bought her expensive presents and admired her beauty. And with one of them, she had fallen in love, and her love had been returned.

'We only had a short time together, but it was blissfully happy,' Dorrie said. 'He had an incurable illness; we knew that from the start, but we were able to live a fairly normal life for quite a long time before the end. He left everything to me. We spent our last holiday together in the Cotswolds and I made up my mind that one day I'd come here to live. And you see, I did.' Tears gathered in her eyes and she fought to keep her voice steady. 'But of course, I knew people would want to know something about me, where I came from and so on. I couldn't tell the truth, so I . . .' Dorrie spread her hands in a mute gesture of embarrassment.

'You invented a Jamaican background, thinking there'd be less chance of anyone spotting that it was phoney?' Melissa gestured at the picture over the mantelpiece. 'I'd be careful about that, if I were you. That's no family heirloom, is it?'

'No, it isn't,' Dorrie admitted. 'How did you know?'

'It's painted in a medium that wasn't invented until this century. Iris spotted it at once.'

'Oh dear.' Dorrie's mouth puckered in dismay. 'She must think me a fool.'

'Never mind that now. You still haven't told me what has upset you so much. As a matter of interest,' Melissa went on as Dorrie seemed reluctant to continue her story, 'when you bought this house, did you know Laura Maddox had come to live in the county?'

'Of course not. I'd have thought twice about it if I had. I knew she once had an aunt who lived in Stowbridge – in fact, I visited her several times with Laura when we were still friends. Laura didn't like her aunt, but she kept in with her because she hoped to inherit her property. I suppose that's what happened – but Laura hated Stowbridge. I never dreamed she'd live anywhere but London.'

'I don't suppose she ever intended to move down here, but maybe she didn't have much choice after her father went to gaol.'

This last remark evoked another sharp glance from

Dorrie and she seemed about to ask a question, but instead switched her attention back to her restless hands. During the recital, her carefully cultivated 'genteel' accent had gradually slipped away and she had become once again the vulnerable girl from London's East End, floundering in an alien world. For several seconds she was silent.

'Look, Dorrie,' Melissa said at length, 'when are you going to come to the point? Exactly why did you ask me here? Is it because Laura has run you to earth and is threatening to tell the world about your past if you don't share your inheritance with her? Because if she is, it's blackmail and you should go to the police. But you know that already, don't you?'

Dorrie seemed to crumple. She bowed her head, hunched her shoulders and covered her face with her hands. She shrank back in her chair like a child pretending to be invisible.

'Oh, dear God, I wish it was that. If only it was that,' she moaned.

'Whatever do you mean?'

The only response was a series of stifled sobs. Melissa's patience gave out; she jumped from her chair and pulled Dorrie's hands away from her face. 'What exactly has happened?' she demanded.

Dorrie stared up at her with terror in her eyes. Words and phrases began spilling from her mouth in breathless jerks. 'I went to see Laura . . . I hoped we could . . . come to some arrangement . . . maybe I'd have made her an allowance . . . if she was as hard up as she said . . . for old times' sake . . . although knowing what she was like, she'd always have been coming back for more.' During the last sentence her voice became steadier and the final words were spat out in a tone filled with venom. Her mouth set momentarily in a hard, bitter line.

'So what happened when you got there?' Melissa asked, and the look of terror returned.

'I knocked several times but she didn't answer. Then I remembered where her aunt used to hide a spare key so I went round the back of the house to see if it was still there. I didn't need it, though . . . the door was open. I went in and called, but no one answered. Then I went up to her bedroom and found her.' Dorrie gagged and put a hand to her mouth. 'It was gruesome!' she whispered.

Melissa felt a sensation like cold water being sprayed over several parts of her body at once. 'You mean, she was dead?'

Dorrie's face worked and she gasped for breath, as if the memory had rushed up like a tidal wave and swamped her. 'She was in her bed and there was a terrible smell and . . .' Dorrie covered her eyes and it was several seconds before she continued, almost inaudibly, unaware of the effect her words were having on her listener. 'Someone had drawn on her face with lipstick . . . an awful, hideous smile.' She lowered her hands and stared helplessly at Melissa. 'What shall I do?' she said piteously. 'The police will think I murdered her!'

It took a while for Dorrie to became calm enough to fill in the details. Laura had played her hand very cleverly at first; she had written a letter to her 'dear old friend', expressing delight that they were living so close to one another and hoping that they would soon be able to get together and chat about old times. She had given her telephone number and asked Dorrie – or rather, Daisy – to call her, which she had of course done, terrified that if she did not, she would receive an unwelcome and potentially embarrassing visit. During the conversation Laura had made no overt threats, but congratulated her former protégée on her good fortune, contrasting it with her own reduced circumstances, inviting her to visit her humble abode . . . and hinting that the visit might be returned.

'She sounded as sweet as honey; no one listening in would ever have dreamed there was anything threatening behind what she was saying,' Dorrie said. 'But I knew what she was after all right . . . I knew what she was really like, you see. If I didn't play along, she'd humiliate me before all my friends – and enjoy it.'

'She certainly didn't show much honey sweetness when I first met her,' said Melissa drily. 'Although she was dripping it all over her boyfriend when I saw her later. He was lapping it up.'

Dorrie gave a little snort of contempt. 'Her latest toy boy, I suppose! That's where my money would have gone, if I'd given her any.' Dorrie broke off with an irritable gesture. 'I'm sorry, I'm getting side-tracked.'

'Let me get this straight,' said Melissa, whose thoughts had been running in a direction that would have astonished Dorrie. 'When did you last speak to Laura?'

'I've only spoken to her once, last Friday.'

'And when did you arrange to meet?'

'Yesterday evening. She invited me for supper.'

'When I heard her shouting after you, she was saying something about finding out where you live. Would that have been a problem?'

'I asked her about that. My number's not in the book and in any case the name Grantley-Newcombe would mean nothing to her. I invented it, you see.'

'And what did she say?'

'She gave one of her silly laughs and said something about little boys having their uses. What d'you suppose she meant by that?'

'I've no idea,' said Melissa untruthfully, while her mind went racing ahead. It was not difficult to deduce how Laura had come by the information she needed to track down Daisy Grice, and it was a fair assumption that her motive in doing so had been to relieve her 'old friend' of large sums of money.

Assuming that Dorrie was telling the truth – and Melissa had no reason to believe otherwise – Laura was known to be alive on Friday evening, when the 'Daughters of Light' were still at liberty. It sounded as if she had been dead for some time when Dorrie found her, which meant that she could have been their latest victim – although, since she was neither old nor frail, she was hardly the type to attract their attention. But if they had not killed her, it must have been someone familiar with their methods. Which, in Melissa's mind, pointed inexorably in one direction. In any event, the next step was obvious.

'You have to go to the police. You must,' Melissa insisted as Dorrie vehemently shook her head. 'Her body's going to be found sooner or later – in fact, it may already have been reported and a murder hunt started. Did you use your car to visit her house?' Dorrie nodded. 'It's a very distinctive car; someone's sure to have seen it and it'll be traced back to you. It's in your own interests.'

Dorrie appeared to be about to raise more objections, but at that moment they heard the sound of wheels on the gravelled drive. Both women glanced out of the window;

Dorrie gave a cry of terror as a car drew up outside the front door and a man and a woman got out.

'They're here already . . . they know about it! Oh God, what shall I do?' She clutched at Melissa's arm. 'Help me!' she begged.

'Shsh . . . calm down. We don't know for certain that they're police officers,' said Melissa, but she was aware that her voice lacked conviction.

'Supposing they are? Do I have to answer their questions?'

'It'll look fishy if you don't.'

'But I haven't done anything wrong,' Dorrie wailed.

'Then you've nothing to be afraid of, have you?'

Chapter Nineteen

'Will you see what they want, Melissa?' Dorrie begged. 'I must go and see to my make-up and . . .'

'And top up with speed, I suppose,' Melissa muttered under her breath as Dorrie, leaving the sentence unfinished, darted from the room. She followed her into the hall, gave her time to disappear upstairs and then opened the front door. In the porch stood a middle-aged man wearing an anorak and dark trousers, and a younger woman in a raincoat.

'Mrs Grantley-Newcombe?' said the man.

'No, I'm just a visitor. Who wants her?'

'DC Belling and DC Simpson, Gloucestershire Constabulary.' The two displayed their warrant cards.

'You'd better come in. I'll tell Mrs Grantley-Newcombe you're here.'

Melissa, who was still feeling shaken by the latest twist to the chronicle of death that had sent shock waves across the county, ushered the visitors into the room where, only a short time ago, she had learned of the gruesome fate of Laura Maddox. She hoped that her manner, as she invited them to sit down, betrayed no sign of agitation; her main anxiety was for Dorrie, who was far more affected. It would be obvious to a trained eye that she was hiding something. However much or little she revealed under this preliminary questioning, further enquiries would be set afoot and the history of her relationship with the dead woman would almost certainly come to light. Her hopes of maintaining her charade could be rated as very slender indeed.

With these thoughts running through her head, Melissa went upstairs, half-expecting to find Dorrie in a state of distress. She was taken aback to meet her on the landing, looking composed and feigning mild curiosity about the visitors. When Melissa informed her of their identity, in a voice deliberately pitched to enable them to hear, she swept downstairs and greeted them with a gracious smile.

'What can I do for you? I haven't been caught speeding, have I?' she said brightly.

The transformation was remarkable. She had evidently summoned up all her experience of playing the rôle of escort to her many sophisticated clients in order to present an unconcerned, self-possessed image. Melissa's admiration for her courage was tempered with anxiety; how many pills had she taken to produce this effect in so short a time?

'No, Madam, it isn't anything like that,' DC Belling assured her. 'We're here to ask if you can help with our enquiries on another matter.' He consulted his notebook. 'You are Mrs Dorinda Grantley-Newcombe?'

'That's right. Do sit down . . . would you like some coffee? Melissa, would you mind awfully . . . ?'

'No coffee, thank you Madam. If I could just ask you one or two questions.'

'Of course.' Dorrie sank gracefully into a chair and Melissa sat down as well, but the detectives, who had risen when the women entered, remained standing.

'You are the owner of a dark green Jaguar, registration . . .' Belling consulted his notebook again and read out Dorrie's cherished personal number.

'That's right.' She gave a quick frown of apparent alarm. 'It hasn't been involved in an accident, has it?'

'Not that I know of. Do I take it the vehicle is not on the premises at the moment?'

'One of my employees, Tony Barnard, has taken it out on an errand. He should be back shortly. But why . . . ?' Her expression of innocent enquiry would have earned praise from the most critical of drama teachers.

'Who besides you and Mr Barnard drives the car?'

'No one else.'

'I see. Now,' the detective consulted his notebook yet again, 'which of you was in charge of the car yesterday evening between approximately six and seven o'clock?'

'I was. I went out about half-past five and didn't get back until gone eleven.'

'And where were you between the times I mentioned?'

Dorrie reached for a cigarette from a silver box on a low table at her elbow. It was the first time Melissa had seen her smoke; she guessed that her purpose was to give herself a few seconds to think.

'Let me see, now. Yes, of course, I was in Grafton Street, Stowbridge, but only for a few minutes around six o'clock.'

'What were you doing there?'

'I was calling on a friend.'

'Would that be a lady called Laura Maddox who lives at number forty-two?'

Dorrie's start of surprise was no more pronounced than would be expected from someone who thinks their mind has been read.

'Why, yes?' she said. 'How did you know?'

'The car was seen parked outside her house at the time we're speaking of,' said Belling.

'Well, there's no secret about it.' Dorrie leaned back in her chair, her cigarette held between fingers that trembled only slightly. *Full marks for nerve, but how long can she keep it up?* Melissa wondered. 'I went to see her, but there was no reply to my knock and the house was in darkness,' Dorrie explained between puffs.

'So you concluded she was out?'

Dorrie took a longer draw on her cigarette and expelled the smoke through her nostrils. 'It seemed a logical assumption,' she said casually.

'Were you expecting her to be there?'

'Yes, actually, I was. She'd invited me to call that evening . . . at least,' Dorrie gave a slight giggle, 'I *thought* it was that evening, but she was always a bit vague about dates and times so we must have got it mixed up. I knocked two or three times and then I came away.'

The detective gave no sign that he had noticed her unconscious use of the past tense. 'Have you tried to contact her since?' he asked.

'No. I've been meaning to, but I've been rather busy. Mrs Craig and I,' she glanced at Melissa as if inviting confirmation, 'have been discussing arrangements for the Nearly New sale in aid of the Friends of Stowbridge Hospital. Officer,' Dorrie assumed a puzzled expression for which Melissa mentally awarded her an Alpha plus, 'what is this about?'

DC Simpson, the young woman officer, spoke for the first time. 'Was Ms Maddox a close friend of yours, Madam?' she asked.

'Not exactly close. An old acquaintance, you could

say. We hadn't seen one another or been in touch for ages when we met accidentally in Cheltenham and discovered we were living quite near to one another.' Dorrie managed a light laugh. 'Such a coincidence; we're both from London originally.' Suddenly, her expression underwent a dramatic change. 'Was? Did you say *was* she my friend? Has something happened to her?'

'Ms Maddox's body was discovered late last night at her home in Grafton Street,' said DC Simpson. She paused for a moment before adding gently, 'I'm afraid this is a murder enquiry.'

'Murder!' Dorrie's hand flew to her mouth in what seemed a wholly natural gesture. 'Laura . . . murdered?' She gave a little cry, sank back in her chair and covered her face. Melissa darted forward, rescued the remains of the cigarette and stubbed it out in an ashtray.

'I'm afraid you've given her quite a shock,' she told the detectives as Dorrie's shoulders began heaving and muffled sobs emerged from behind her hands.

'I take it you weren't acquainted with Ms Maddox yourself?' said Belling.

'Not personally,' said Melissa, remembering that she, too, would be expected to show some reaction to what, so far as the detectives were concerned, was totally unexpected news. 'It's a dreadful thing to hear about just the same.' She made a show of giving all her attention to Dorrie, who was still weeping. The sobs sounded genuine; maybe it was partly relief at not having to keep up her act any longer.

'I really think Mrs Grantley-Newcombe should go to her room and lie down,' Melissa went on. 'If you want to ask her any more questions, perhaps you could come back another time, when she's feeling better.'

'Yes, we'll do that,' Belling agreed. The detectives exchanged nods and moved towards the door. 'You look after her, Mrs Craig, we'll see ourselves out.'

Coincident with the sound of the front door closing, Dorrie's sobs began to subside; by the time the police car started up and drove away she appeared almost completely calm. Melissa looked at her accusingly. 'Was that outburst put on for their benefit?' she asked. 'I thought you were really upset.'

Dorrie gave a sly smirk. 'I am, of course, but not so much as I made out. After all, I was beginning to get over the shock – thanks to you,' she added gratefully.

'Me and a few more pep-pills?' Melissa suggested dryly.

'Why not? I couldn't appear upset *before* I heard the news, could I? Of course,' Dorrie went on, 'when you come to think about it, no one deserved a sticky end more than Laura.' She got up, lit another cigarette and began blowing smoke rings, while Melissa watched her with a mixture of astonishment at her panache and unease at what it might conceal. Just for a second, when describing how she found Laura's body, Dorrie had revealed a searing hatred of the dead woman. There was no doubt that there was more than one facet to her character; the ambitious social climber, so despised by Mrs Bonnet and her like, was a natural survivor who had clawed her way up from the gutter and had no intention of returning to it. She had been badly shaken by her ghastly discovery, but already she was beginning to bounce back. Perhaps it had dawned on her that whoever had been responsible for the death of Laura Maddox had done a very good turn for Dorinda Grantley-Newcombe, formerly Daisy Grice.

Melissa decided to offer a word of warning. 'I don't

want to sound alarmist,' she said, 'but if I were you, I'd have a word with your solicitor before the detectives come back.'

Dorrie's complacent expression changed to one of alarm.

'Come back? Why are they coming back?' she asked hoarsely.

'To ask you some more questions about Laura. You've spoken to her recently; you may know something that could lead them to her killer.'

'But I don't, I don't know anything.' There was nothing artificial about Dorrie's agitation now. 'I hadn't seen her for years, so how could I possibly . . . ?'

'Look Dorrie, just face up to it; they'll be back. It doesn't mean they suspect you, and neither do I,' she went on as Dorrie opened her carefully lipsticked mouth to make a further protest, 'but the fact is, you knew her from way back. It's quite possible you could help them with their enquiries.'

'Well, I don't want to help them,' Dorrie exclaimed in a burst of angry bitterness. 'She was a nasty piece of work and she deserved to be sent down with her father. She managed to wriggle out of that one, but she's got her come uppance now, hasn't she?'

'I wouldn't let the police hear you talk like that,' warned Melissa. 'Besides, to be fair, it's partly due to her and her father that you're living in this house, isn't it?'

'I suppose so,' Dorrie admitted grudgingly.

'The sensible thing to do now is talk to your solicitor about damage limitation. You don't want the press to get hold of your story, do you?'

Dorrie looked appalled at the prospect. 'Oh, my God,'

she whispered. 'I'd have to move . . . I'd never be able to look the people round here in the face again.'

'Then get some professional advice right away.'

'I will. Melissa, I can't thank you enough for coming, and for being so sympathetic. I haven't any real friends here except Tony and Florence . . . they worked for Alex for many years and they stayed on with me after he died.' For once, Dorrie seemed to be speaking with complete sincerity, with no attempt to act a part or create an impression.

'Do they know about this?'

'No, thank goodness. I didn't go straight home after finding Laura's body; I drove around for ages until I'd calmed down. I'd already told Florence I wouldn't be back for dinner, so I was able to slip in and go straight to bed without seeing her.'

'That's just as well.' Melissa got up to leave. 'I'm glad I've been of some help. You make that phone call. I'll be in touch again when I've collected some more things for the sale.'

Melissa's thoughts on the way home were confused. Her advice had been given with Dorrie's best interests in mind; it would be cruel if the violent death of someone from her unhappy past were to bring about the destruction of everything she had fought so hard to achieve. She had given little or no thought to her own position and the detectives had shown no interest in her during the interview, but her presence would have been noted. There could of course be more than one Melissa Craig in the neighbourhood, but the chances were that someone at the police station – Matt Waters, for example – would spot the name and a check would immediately be made.

It was clear that she was faced with an uncomfortable choice. Dorrie had not thought to ask for a promise of silence, but Melissa had no doubt that she had naively taken it for granted. To break her confidence would seem like a betrayal, yet if she herself were questioned, it would be impossible to respect it without lying to the police. Dorrie was a material witness and her presence on the scene of the crime was bound to come to light sooner or later. If Melissa were to conceal what she knew until the truth came out through another line of enquiry, she would be putting herself in an invidious position to no purpose.

'Let's hope,' she muttered aloud as she let herself into Hawthorn Cottage, 'Dorrie's had the sense to take my advice. A smart lawyer might at least be able to prevent the tabloids getting hold of her story.'

The mid-day radio news carried a report of the discovery of Laura Maddox's body and announced that a man was being questioned in connection with her death. No name was mentioned, but there was no doubt in Melissa's mind of the man's identity.

Chapter Twenty

'It's Clifford Fenn, isn't it?' said Melissa, looking up from the Wednesday evening edition of the *Gazette*.

Ken Harris, engrossed in peeling the foil cap from a bottle of Australian Chardonnay, did not look up. 'What about Clifford Fenn?' he asked.

'The man who's been arrested for Laura Maddox's murder.'

He gave her a sharp look. 'Who told you that?'

'No one. I figured it out for myself.'

He uncorked the wine and sniffed at the neck of the bottle. 'This seems okay. How about some glasses?'

Melissa took two goblets from a cupboard and put them on the kitchen table. 'Well?' she said impatiently.

With maddening deliberation, he tipped a small quantity of the straw-coloured wine into one of the glasses and sampled it. Then he poured two generous measures and handed one to her. 'Try that,' he said.

She sniffed, then tasted. 'It's good. Where did you get it?'

'From a client, a wine shipper whose office I debugged, thus helping him to nail an industrial spy. He sent round half a dozen bottles to show his appreciation.' Ken took a mouthful, swallowed, and nodded approval. 'That'll go nicely with the smoked salmon.'

'We're not having smoked salmon.'

'Oh yes, we are.' He produced a packet from a holdall and began slitting it open with a kitchen knife. 'What's to follow?'

'Spiced chicken breasts and a stir-fry. I organised something quick and easy as I had a feeling you'd be late. Getting the latest on the Maddox case from one of your contacts,' she added in response to his raised eyebrow, 'and you still haven't answered my question.'

He shook his head dismissively. 'Look Mel, if you're thinking of worming the gory details out of me, forget it. This is one case where anything I pick up before it's officially released is in the strictest confidence.'

'All right.' Melissa sprinkled Cajun seasoning on the chicken breasts and set them under the grill. 'Let me give you my theory. Clifford Fenn is Laura's latest toy boy, but his days are numbered. Maybe his successor is already lined up, but there's one more thing she wants from him before ditching him.'

'Such as?' prompted Ken, as she broke off to fetch the frying-pan.

'Daisy Grice's address. It's not in the phone book, not even under her assumed name of Dorinda Grantley-Newcombe, which Laura in any case doesn't know. All she has to go on is the car registration number, which is very distinctive and easy to remember. She might have thought of trying to get it from the licensing authority by making up a phoney report of the car being involved in a road accident and failing to stop, but there's no guarantee that they'll fall for it. In any case there's a much more reliable way to hand. Her pet copper, her Cliffie, who'll do anything for her in exchange for a bit of leg-over, will find it for her next time he has a chance to log on to the Police

National Computer.' In the act of tipping the prepared vegetables into the pan, Melissa shot a sidelong glance at Ken; his face gave nothing away. 'Right so far?'

'No comment. Go on.'

'Somehow he managed to get the information she wanted, presumably without anyone's knowledge – although it probably came out when the police were checking on the same car after it was seen outside Laura's house the evening before her body was discovered. Who found her, by the way?'

Ken's voice was as wooden as his expression as he replied, 'That information hasn't been released yet.'

She stared at him accusingly. 'But I'll bet you know.'

'Never mind that now. Go on with your theory.'

Melissa scowled at him in exasperation, then shrugged and turned back to the stir-fry. 'Laura wouldn't of course have told Clifford her real reason for wanting to trace Daisy – she probably fed him some cock-and-bull story about looking up a long-lost friend.'

Until this point, Ken had been listening with an air of detachment, but with a hint of I-know-something-you-don't in his eye. Now his expression changed to one of close attention.

'And what was the real reason?' he asked.

'I'll come to that in a moment. Anyway, Laura's got what she wants from Cliffie so she ditches him. Being absolutely besotted with her, he takes it very badly and goes to her house to plead with her. Perhaps he sees the new lover leaving, or catches them *in flagrante delicto*, or maybe she simply taunts him with the fact that he's served his purpose and has been supplanted. He loses his rag and kills her.'

'And that's it?'

'Not quite.' Melissa checked the grill, gave the sizzling vegetables a final stir and sprinkled them with soy sauce. 'Will you dole out the smoked salmon while I dish up this lot? There's a lemon in the fridge and you know where to find the bread and butter.'

He fetched plates and cutlery and did as she asked. She put the cooked food in the oven to keep hot and sat down at the kitchen table, nursing her wineglass. All of a sudden, she felt less interested in food. 'Now comes the nasty bit,' she said and saw his expression alter yet again.

'He must have killed Laura some time on Friday, probably quite late,' she said slowly, thinking aloud. 'At that time, no one had been arrested for the Thanebury murders so he hit on the idea of making her look like another of the Smiler's victims. He'd have known about the smile, of course; he must have seen photographs taken at the scene of the other killings. There's bound to have been a lipstick in her room, so he . . .' Melissa passed a hand across her eyes in a futile effort to erase the sickening picture, then looked Ken full in the face. 'Am I right?'

'How the hell do you know all this?' he demanded.

'Dorrie – Daisy Grice – found Laura's body early yesterday evening and went into a flat spin, thinking she'd be a suspect because Laura had been threatening to blackmail her – that was why she got Clifford Fenn to track her down. Dorrie drove around in a panic for several hours, spent a sleepless night and rang me this morning to ask me what she should do.'

'Blackmail her?' It was evident from the way his eyebrows shot up that this was something new to the ex-policeman. 'I don't get it.'

'Laura befriended Daisy Grice when she was practically down and out, and introduced her to her father. She was more or less forced to become one of Papa Maddox's toms, but she escaped when she formed a permanent relationship with one of the wealthy clients. That's where her money came from, and Laura wanted a share.'

'And what advice did you give her?' asked Ken, after digesting this information.

'To contact her solicitor and then the police.'

'She's already been interviewed by two detectives – but I suppose you know that as well. I assume you are the "Mrs Craig" who was present while they were questioning her?'

'That's right. They arrived just as I was telling her she should go to them. They didn't take much notice of me until Dorrie got hysterical on being told that Laura had been murdered. She put on a terrific act, by the way – I couldn't help admiring her.' For a second or two, Melissa relived the memory of the beautiful, desperate woman, putting up such a doughty struggle to preserve her standing in society, and felt ashamed at having betrayed her secret. 'Ken, does her past have to come out? Being the lady of the manor means so much to her.'

'I daresay Laura Maddox's life meant a lot to her as well.' Ken's face was expressionless as he cut a lemon into wedges. 'Are we eating here or in the dining room?'

'In here, I think, if that's okay with you.'

'It's fine.' He put the plates of fish on the table and set out knives and forks. 'So what happened when her ladyship went into hysterics?'

'The detectives left me to look after her, but said they'd

want to talk to her again. After they'd gone I repeated what I'd said about getting professional advice because of her previous connection with Laura, but I assured her that she wouldn't be a suspect. That seemed to give her some comfort, but what she's every bit as scared of is the story of her past getting into the tabloids.'

'I'd say that was the least of her worries.'

'What do you mean?'

'You obviously haven't thought this through, Mel. From what you've told me, it's plain that Laura's death has come at a very convenient time for Daisy.'

'You aren't suggesting that she killed Laura? She isn't strong enough, and in any case she couldn't possibly have known about the smile.'

'Agreed, but suppose Laura, besides telling Fenn he'd had his chips, had boasted to him about what she intended to do with the information he'd got for her? She sounds that sort of woman. Maybe he decided to warn Daisy. Maybe the two of them hatched a little scheme together; Daisy would call on Laura, take a couple of bottles, suggest they talk it through over a few strong gins. At the end of the evening, Laura staggers up to bed and falls into a drunken stupor – the PM revealed a large amount of alcohol in the body. Daisy lets Fenn into the house and he makes sure Laura never wakes up.'

Melissa's jaw dropped. 'You're right!' she exclaimed, 'that never entered my head.'

'Otherwise, you're on track. Congratulations!' He refilled both their glasses and raised his in salute. 'And first thing tomorrow, you go down to the station and make a full statement about your conversation with Daisy. You might get a rocket from Des Holloway for not going straight away, but I'm sure you can talk him round.'

'I'm not too sure about that,' she replied with a wan smile, 'but Ken, I'm certain you're wrong. Why would Dorrie – Daisy, I mean – confess everything to me if she really had conspired with Fenn?'

'Maybe he warned her that he thought the police were on to him and she concocted the story to cover herself. Or maybe they cooked it up together; she was to pretend to find the body and report it, but chickened out.'

'But in that case . . . oh, I see. It was *Clifford* who reported finding it, wasn't it?'

She looked him full in the eye, challenging him to confirm her guess, but he would not be drawn. 'I'm not giving away any more,' he said. 'Come on, let's have our supper. I'm starving.'

He fell to with relish and did not appear to notice that Melissa, still disturbed by the thought of how Laura had died and unhappy at the knowledge that she had betrayed Dorrie's confidence, ate with less appetite than usual.

All the national papers carried reports of the discovery of the body of Laura Maddox in the bedroom of her house in the small Gloucestershire town of Stowbridge, but most were brief, single-paragraph items tucked away on an inside page. However, an enterprising journalist with a good memory had checked the records and written a sensational piece about the victim's sleazy past. On Friday, the 'exclusive' was splashed on the front page of one of the tabloids, but Melissa, anxiously skimming through the story, was relieved to find no reference to a link between the daughter of a convicted procurer and the wealthy Mrs Dorinda Grantley-Newcombe of Carston Manor.

'Not that that means anything,' Melissa remarked,

throwing the paper aside to accept a glass of fruit juice from Iris. 'Once the *paparazzi* pick up the scent of a scandal, they'll hunt poor Dorrie down like a pack of hyenas.'

'Any reason why they should pick it up?' asked Iris, settling on the garden bench beside her. She pushed the sleeves of her shapeless sweater up to her elbows, revealing thin brown arms. 'Who's to know that Dorrie knew Laura, or that she's really Daisy Grice?'

'True, provided . . .' Just in time, Melissa remembered having promised Ken to keep yesterday's developments, and their joint theories, to herself for the time being.

'Provided what?' Iris was instantly alert and Melissa avoided meeting her sharp grey eyes.

'I don't know,' she prevaricated, 'once they start scratching around, there's no telling what they'll dig up.'

'Dorrie'll think of something to put 'em off. We know how inventive she is, don't we? Wonder how she's taken this.' Iris jabbed a finger at the newspaper.

'I wonder.'

'Anyway,' Iris drank her juice, put down the glass and locked her hands behind her head, 'it sounds as if they've got the man who did it. Quick work, that.' She gave one of her witch-like cackles. 'Five murders solved in one week; that'll please the Home Secretary no end.'

Melissa chuckled, then turned the conversation to safer topics. It was an exceptionally mild, early April afternoon and the sheltered south-facing patio outside Elder Cottage was bathed in sunshine. Having spent a couple of hours working in their gardens, the two were enjoying a break. As they sat contentedly exchanging idle chat and watching the activities of the local bird and insect population, Sirry Donovan appeared.

She was wearing a strikingly patterned sweater and well-cut slacks that flattered her figure, and her glossy hair, hanging loose about her shoulders, gleamed with coppery tints in the sunlight. She gave one of the brilliant smiles with which she and her sister had charmed most of the residents of Upper Benbury and said, 'What a lovely day!'

Iris indicated a spare seat. 'Sit down. Like a drink?'

Sirry shook her head. 'No thank you, we're just going out. I called round to invite you both to tea tomorrow.'

'Thanks. Love to,' said Iris. 'How about you Mel?'

'Well, thank you, but Ken Harris will probably be here,' Melissa began, but Sirry cut in.

'Oh please, bring your friend as well. Father hasn't had a man to talk to for ages. He's so much better, largely thanks to you, Iris. We thought it was time we had a bit more company in the house.'

Not for the first time, Melissa reflected with sympathy on the restricted lives the sisters had been leading since their brother's death. For two attractive young women to spend their days cooped up with an eccentric, difficult father in an out-of-the-way village seemed unnatural. They always seemed reasonably content – and of course Genty had her part-time job at the art college – but surely there must be times when they longed to be free of the responsibility. If only their mother had not left home, things might have been easier for them. Perhaps she would return now; perhaps this was the start of happier times for the whole family.

'See you tomorrow then, say about four?' said Sirry.

'Looking forward to it,' Iris replied and Melissa nodded and smiled in agreement.

'I hope Ken won't mind,' she remarked after Sirry had left. 'He might think it's a pretty tame way to spend a Saturday afternoon.'

'Might welcome a rest from chasing after crooks.' Iris either could not, or would not be bothered to grasp the difference between the work of a policeman and a private investigator. She got up and flexed her arms and fingers. 'Feeling a bit stiff after all that gardening. Think I'll do some yoga.'

Chapter Twenty-One

The moment Melissa arrived at Larkfield Barn, in company with Iris and Ken, she sensed a lightening of the atmosphere. There was a quiet radiance about the Donovan sisters as they showed their guests into the cosy sitting-room, where the afternoon sunshine pouring through the mullioned windows echoed the warmth of their welcome. She glanced at Ken, saw his nod of appreciation and knew that he shared her impression.

'Father will be with us in a minute,' said Genty, and as she spoke, Cluny entered. There was a subtle change about him also; he appeared taller than Melissa remembered and she realised that there had previously been a droop to his head and shoulders that was no longer evident.

'Welcome, welcome!' he cried, shaking hands all round. 'Sit down, sit down!' he urged with a sweep of one hand while resting the other on the mantelpiece where, Melissa noticed with a slight *frisson*, candles in silver holders had been lit on either side of the portrait of his son and a bowl of fresh spring flowers placed between them.

'Wasn't the boy like his father!' whispered Ken in Melissa's ear as they sat down in adjacent chairs. 'It's uncanny.'

Iris, meanwhile, having briefly considered the hearth-rug, settled for the couch. Cluny promptly placed himself at her side.

‘ ’Tis good to see you, me darling,’ he said, patting her hand. ‘And what are you working on just now?’

‘Fabric designs for the autumn,’ she replied. ‘Care to come and see them?’

‘ ’Twould be a pleasure.’ He patted her hand again. ‘I’ll come tomorrow.’

‘What about you?’ Iris challenged him with a sharp look. ‘When am I going to see some work in progress?’

‘Soon, soon, I hope.’ For a moment, the old sorrow seemed to drift round his head and shoulders like a mourning veil; then it was gone as he said brightly, ‘I’d like you to see some of me daughter’s work, though. Genty me darling, why don’t you show Iris the sketches you’ve been doing?’

Genty looked faintly embarrassed. ‘Oh, some other time, Father. Our guests didn’t come to look at my scribbles,’ she protested.

‘Don’t be so modest, girl,’ Cluny insisted and the guests made politely encouraging noises, but Genty was adamant.

‘Not now,’ she said firmly. ‘Sirry, come and help me with the tea-things.’

Sirry obediently followed her sister into the kitchen; the minute they had gone, Cluny sprang to his feet. ‘Back in a minute,’ he said, and disappeared through a door in the far corner of the room, returning seconds later with a portfolio in his hands. ‘Too modest by half is me younger daughter,’ he said. ‘Inherited her old father’s gift, so she has. Her brother did too, God rest his soul.’ Again, sorrow momentarily clouded the old man’s eyes and he glanced up at the portrait which, flanked by flowers and candles, seemed to have taken on the mystical quality of an icon. For the second time, Melissa felt a faint tingling sensation on her skin. Ken and Iris had followed Cluny's glance and she sensed that they too were affected as they heard him murmur, 'Rest in peace, my son,' before unfastening the portfolio.

He seemed to be having trouble with the tapes and Iris got up to help. After a brief tussle, the knots gave way and the portfolio flew open, scattering its contents on the floor. Everyone began helping to retrieve them, while Cluny tutted in exasperation.

''Tis the wrong one I've brought . . . this must be her students' work. I'll put this lot away and fetch the other. Holy Mother of God, what's this?' He gazed in stupefaction at the single sheet of white cartridge paper in his hand and the others moved forward to look at it. Iris gave a faint gasp and Melissa clapped a hand over her mouth to stifle a cry.

Someone had executed a vague pencil impression of the head of an old woman lying on a lace-edged pillow. Sparse, wispy hair trailed over hollow cheeks, the toothless mouth hung open and the sunken eyes were wide and staring, their gaze fixed in the rigid emptiness of death. In the bottom right-hand corner was the signature, 'Natalie'. The drawing had been executed with some skill, but no one had eyes for anything but the pair of thick, hideously smiling lips superimposed on it in scarlet wax crayon.

Melissa felt as if there was ice in her bloodstream. She took a deep breath and clutched at Ken's hand. Iris looked faintly disgusted, but the glance she gave Melissa revealed that the significance of the embellishment had not been lost on her. Ken's face was impassive as he peered over Cluny's shoulder.

In silence, apparently unaware of the effect it was having on his guests, the artist studied the drawing with an air of professional appraisal before throwing it to one side without further comment and returning to the task of gathering up the remaining contents of the portfolio. Mechanically, the others followed suit. It was Iris's turn to give a grunt of surprise as she picked up a sheet covered in half a dozen smaller, less detailed representations of the gruesome subject.

'Must be sick,' she commented as she passed it to Cluny. He held the two sheets side by side and considered them with the same critical air as before. Melissa turned to Ken and opened her mouth to speak, but he put a finger to his lips and then pointed to the drawings. 'May I?' he said.

'By all means.' Cluny handed them over.

Ken examined them closely before returning them. 'What's your opinion?' he asked.

'I'm blest if I know,' said Cluny, shaking his head. 'Natalie, whoever she is, seems to be trying to copy something she's seen – something by Francis Bacon, maybe. I don't care for it meself, but the girl has talent. I see she did some practice first.' He gestured with the sheet of multiple drawings and gave an approving nod. He half turned as Sirry entered with a tray of tea-things. 'I don't know what inspired this peculiar subject,' he said, 'but your sister evidently passes on her old Dad's advice to her students. Practice makes perfect, isn't that what I've always said?' With a hoarse chuckle, he put the drawings on the table and held out both hands to relieve Sirry of the tray. 'Here girl, give me that. Where are you wanting it now?'

He did not appear to notice Sirry's expression of dismay on seeing the drawings, nor the startled look that flitted across her sister's face as, seconds later, she entered with the teapot in one hand and a kettle in the other.

'Oh Father!' Genty exclaimed reproachfully. 'Whatever possessed you to bring those out?' She set the kettle on the hearth and the teapot on the table. 'What makes you think my students' work is of interest to anyone here.'

''Twas a mistake, me darling. I thought 'twas your own portfolio,' Cluny explained. 'I just wanted our guests to see what a talented daughter I have.'

'It doesn't matter,' said Genty, busy setting out cups and saucers. 'Put them away now, do.'

Despite the sickening reaction they evoked in her, Melissa could not take her eyes from the drawings that still lay where Cluny had dropped them. From the turmoil seething in her memory, a question flew to the surface and was uttered before she could check it. Her voice was unsteady as she asked, 'Genty, are those Natalie's doodles – the ones you were telling me about?'

'That's right,' Genty replied calmly. 'When I first saw them, I honestly thought something had turned her brain, but she told me that's how the dead woman looked when she found her. Horrible, isn't it? No wonder the poor girl was traumatised. She made me swear not to tell a living soul.'

'What about the large drawing? That's hardly a doodle,' Ken remarked.

'I suggested she should make a more detailed study of what she'd seen . . . I thought it might help to exorcise the memory. A sort of catharsis, I suppose . . . but it didn't work. In fact, it nearly led to tragedy.'

'How do you mean?' asked Ken.

'Didn't you hear what she did a few days later? You can't imagine how guilty I felt.' Genty's expression was sombre as she picked up the drawings, slid them into the portfolio and put it aside. 'Let's not talk about it any more.' She had been setting out cups and saucers as she spoke. 'Sirry, will you pass round the cakes? Does everyone take milk in their tea?'

No wonder she seemed nervous at the prospect of coming face to face with Natalie after her suicide attempt, thought Melissa as she accepted tea and cake, while Cluny turned the conversation to less disturbing topics. *I'd love to be able to tell her about the pressure the 'Daughters of Light' put on that poor girl. It might set her mind at rest – I must have a word with Ken when we get home.*

It was while these thoughts were running through Melissa's head that something else occurred to her, setting her brain on a different track.

'Genty, you told me about the doodles, but I understood you'd never seen them,' she said.

'Did I say that?' For a moment, Genty appeared disconcerted, but quickly recovered. 'Well, of course, I had promised not to talk about them . . . and besides, they're so horrible that I didn't really want to – although they do show signs of talent, don't you agree, Father?'

'Oh, certainly,' Cluny agreed. 'And as you see, she'd done all that practice beforehand.' The significance of the drawings had totally escaped him; he smiled and wagged a forefinger as he pronounced his favourite maxim. 'Practice makes perfect. Haven't I always said so?' His daughters responded with their usual nods of agreement, but for once their smiles seemed forced.

The awkward silence that followed was broken by Ken Harris. 'You said it was at your suggestion that Natalie made that detailed study of the dead woman?' he said to Genty.

'That's right,' she agreed. 'I suppose I shouldn't have done it . . . I mean, it would have been better for her to have expert psychiatric advice, but she wouldn't hear of it, wouldn't speak about her experience to anyone but me. Although she didn't actually *say* anything . . . it was all done with the drawings.'

'And she did the large one shortly before her suicide attempt?'

'Suicide . . . what suicide?' demanded Cluny. At last it seemed to be dawning on him that the others knew something of which he was unaware.

Ken gestured in the direction of the portfolio. 'The girl who did those rather unpleasant drawings tried to kill herself about ten days ago.'

Cluny looked shocked. 'May God forgive her! What possessed her to do such a terrible thing?' he said.

'She was in a very depressed state,' Ken replied. He turned back to Genty. 'Can you remember when Natalie gave you the drawings?'

'Quite recently – I don't know exactly. She showed me the doodles first, and that was when I suggested she do the more detailed study.'

Ken got to his feet and fetched the portfolio. A silence fell on the room as he took out the larger drawing and showed it to Genty. 'It's dated the fifteenth of January,' he said quietly. 'There,' he pointed with a stubby forefinger, 'concealed in the detail of the lace.'

Genty's face had suddenly lost most of its colour and her voice was pitched a little higher than normal as she observed, 'Bless the child, what a place to put it! Perhaps it was a subconscious attempt to hide the experience away.

That must be the date when she found the body of Miss Twigg.'

'No,' Ken contradicted her. So far, he had been asking his questions in a tone of mild, almost casual interest, but now his voice took on a more deliberate quality as he said, 'Miss Twigg had been dead just a week when this drawing was made. Yet you said it was made recently, at your suggestion. Can you explain that?' Melissa could see only his profile, but it was enough to reveal the almost mesmeric stare he was directing at Genty. She felt a sensation of cold in the pit of her stomach. The room had become very quiet. All eyes were on Ken Harris; Iris's sharp with interest, Cluny's frankly puzzled, Genty's defensive and Sirry's wide with apprehension.

'Will someone please tell me what's going on?' Cluny burst out peevishly. 'We were having a nice tea party – why do we have to bother with these horrid little drawings? And who was Miss Twigg, God rest her soul?'

'She was the third victim of a series of murders committed in Thanebury in recent months,' Harris told him. 'One of your daughter's students discovered her body, the face disfigured as you see it in these pictures. It upset her very much.'

'I'm not surprised,' said Cluny. ''Twould upset a grown man, leave alone a young girl. Now, why don't we put them away and talk about something pleasant?'

'I'm still waiting for an answer to my question,' Harris said. He had not taken his eyes from Genty's face and Melissa could see her growing restless under his implacable gaze.

'I can't explain it,' she said sullenly. 'The girl's unbalanced . . . there's no rational explanation.'

'Oh, but I think there is.' With a sudden movement,

Harris turned from her and sat on the couch beside Cluny. 'I'd like to ask you one or two questions, Mr Donovan, but I'm afraid they may distress you,' he said. 'They concern the death of your son.'

Genty reasserted herself. 'Really, Mr Harris – Ken – aren't you forgetting yourself? What gives you the right to question us like this? You're acting like a policeman.'

'It so happens that I used to be one. I'm now a private investigator and I maintain strong links with the local CID. Perhaps you didn't know that?'

'No, I didn't.' Genty's voice was little more than a whisper.

'Policeman? What are you saying, girl? What have we to do with the police?' demanded Cluny.

'Your daughter's right when she says I have no authority to question you,' Ken said quietly, 'but I have reason to believe that she learned from Natalie something that could be of considerable help to the police in their hunt for a murderer.'

Genty was showing signs of agitation; she was shredding a paper napkin with trembling fingers and there were tiny beads of sweat on her upper lip. Sirry had shrunk back into an armchair and sat motionless as a statue.

'I've already told the police everything that Natalie told me,' Genty went on. 'Please don't pursue this any further, not now, not in front of Father.'

'You didn't show them these drawings, though,' persisted Harris. 'Why not? It's up to you whether you answer my questions now, or whether I pass the drawings to the CID and let them handle it,' he went on as she remained silent. 'Of course, if you can convince me that you really have nothing significant to add, that will be the end of the matter.'

'You said you wanted to ask *me* some questions,' said Cluny testily. 'Why don't you get on with it, now?'

'All right,' said Harris. 'First, do you know a woman called Laura Maddox?'

There was a hiss of indrawn breath. Sirry shut her eyes; Cluny licked his lips and his gaze flickered briefly towards the portrait above the mantelpiece. Genty, who had been sitting on the arm of her sister's chair, went to her father's side and put an arm round his shoulders before replying for all three of them. 'We know of her, yes. Why do you ask?'

'Did Saxe Donovan have a relationship with her?'

Cluny seemed to crumple; his clothes suddenly seemed too large for him and he covered his face with shaking hands. His shoulders heaved. 'She bewitched him, the poor young fool,' he said brokenly. 'Bewitched him, then threw him aside like a broken toy.'

'What happened after that?'

'He went to pieces, got in with the wrong people, turned to drink and drugs for comfort . . . and then he . . .' It was some time before the old man could continue, but presently he mastered his distress and raised his head with the air of one who has found inner strength and comfort. 'It was an accident . . . he never intended to take his own life,' he declared. 'It was his passion for that accursed woman that blinded and destroyed him, but now he can rest in peace, for she is dead, and if there's justice in Heaven she is burning in the everlasting fire.' The final words were pronounced with a fervour that was unnerving in its intensity.

'Who told you that Laura Maddox is dead?' asked Harris.

'Me daughters.' Cluny glanced at the two women, who

sat looking at him as if transfixed. 'They had the news from one of Saxe's old friends. And good riddance, that's what I say. That's what we all say, isn't it me darlings? And we drank champagne to celebrate, and we're not ashamed of it. The world's a better place without that whore.'

'Did your daughters tell you how Laura Maddox died?' Harris asked quietly.

'No, and I didn't ask. I didn't care, don't you understand? She as good as killed my boy and now she's dead herself, and that's good enough for me.' Curiosity got the better of him at last and he added, 'Well, what happened to the bitch?'

'She was murdered.'

'Murdered? Well, I'm not surprised.' Cluny showed no emotion at the news. 'She had it coming to her . . . and if I knew who did it I'd give him a medal!'

'I can sympathise with your feelings,' said Harris, 'but I'm afraid the police will see the matter rather differently. By the way,' he added, as if he had only just thought of the question, 'when did you learn of Laura Maddox's death.'

'That's enough!' Everyone jumped at Genty's intervention. 'Don't say any more Father.' Her face was very white and her hands were trembling. 'Please, Mr Harris . . . everyone . . . I must ask you to leave. This is very distressing for my father . . . for all of us.'

Cluny brushed the protest aside. ''Tis all right, me darling, I can talk about it now,' he said bravely, patting her knee. ''Twas last Saturday morning, the day you went to see that poor girl in the hospital. You had a phone call, and . . .'

'No, you're getting confused, Father.' It was Sirry who

made one last, despairing attempt to avert disaster. 'It was later, Monday, no Tuesday, I think it was . . . we saw it in the paper . . .'

'Confused? That I am not!' said the old man indignantly. 'You and I, Sirry, went to the supermarket after we had the glad news and we bought champagne.' He appealed to Melissa. 'You remember, don't you? You asked me whose birthday we were celebrating?' There was a touch of bravado in his smile as he said, 'It didn't seem right to tell you the real reason, but I don't mind you knowing now.'

Melissa tried to return the smile, but she was close to tears. She could not help but be moved at Cluny's simple-hearted rejoicing at what, to him, was the well-deserved fate of someone who had brought so much misery to himself and his family. With a sense of helpless dread, she waited for the revelation that would shatter their lives forever. She sensed that Ken Harris shared her pity for the old man, that he had to steel himself before saying, in an unusually gentle voice, 'Mr Donovan, I'd like your daughters to explain how they knew of Laura Maddox's death some forty-eight hours before her body was discovered.'

Sirry began to whimper and Genty sat as if turned to stone, while their father looked from one to the other, appalled at what he read in their faces.

'Oh me darlings, what have you done? For pity's sake, what have you done?' he whispered.

No one spoke or stirred as, like a man in a trance, he got up and stood before the portrait of his dead son. For several minutes he gazed at it in silence; then he raised his right hand and deliberately extinguished the candles between a finger and thumb. He leaned both arms on the mantelpiece and bowed his head over them as if in prayer. Like players in the final scene of a tragic masque, his daughters went and stood on either side of him.

'Which of you killed Laura Maddox?' asked Ken. 'Or was it both of you?'

Cluny gave a despairing groan and Sirry began piteously weeping, but Genty swung round and faced their accuser defiantly. There was an almost religious exultation in her gaze; her nostrils flared and her eyes blazed. To Melissa's horror, she gave a peal of mocking laughter.

'We did! Yes, we did!' The words rang out in unholy triumph. 'But you'll never prove it, never! We left no clues, we knew exactly what to do and how to do it. We'd done it before, you see. We'd practised, like Dad always told us! Practice makes perfect! Practice makes perfect!'

It was Iris who moved swiftly forward and slapped Genty sharply round the face to check the hysterics, while Melissa stood helplessly by and Ken Harris, his face grimmer than she had ever seen it, went to the telephone.

Chapter Twenty-Two

'Ken, did you have any idea before our visit to the Donovans that they were involved in the murder of Laura Maddox?' asked Melissa. 'I thought Clifford Fenn was number one suspect.'

It was her first opportunity to question Harris since Genty's frenzied outburst had reduced everyone to a stunned, disbelieving silence, which had continued almost unbroken until the arrival of a team of officers led by Acting Chief Inspector Holloway. On Harris's suggestion – somewhat grudgingly accepted by Holloway – Iris and Melissa had been allowed to go home, accompanied by a policewoman, who took statements from them before rejoining her colleagues. Since then, they had eaten supper in Iris's kitchen and followed it with endless cups of tea while impatiently awaiting news.

Eventually, Harris had arrived at Elder Cottage, looking weary and complaining of hunger. Iris good-naturedly offered to 'rustle up a snack', leaving him with Melissa in the sitting-room. A fire crackled in the hearth, for the April evenings were chilly, and he stretched out his legs in front of the blaze in evident appreciation.

In reply to Melissa's question, he said, 'As far as I know, until this afternoon Fenn was still in the frame because of his relationship with Laura Maddox, but

Waters hinted that the only evidence against him was circumstantial. Then I remembered your telling me that Mrs Grantley-Newcombe had implied that Maddox had a weakness for toy boys.'

'One of whom might have been Saxe Donovan?'

'I didn't think of him immediately, but a couple of days ago I was talking about the case with my ex-colleague in London. He happened to mention that Maddox had been involved for a time with a young artist who'd taken to drugs and generally gone to pieces after she dumped him. It occurred to me then that it could have been young Donovan and for what it was worth, I passed on the tip via Waters. I've no idea if it's been followed up yet, but . . .' He broke off as Iris appeared with a mug of beer and a plate piled high with sandwiches of home-made wholemeal bread. 'Bless you, you're a life-saver,' he said gratefully.

'Mushroom pâté, cottage cheese and celery,' she said, indicating with a finger. 'No meat in this house,' she added with a sly glance at Melissa.

'I'm sure they'll taste wonderful.' He set about demolishing the food with enthusiasm. 'Sorry I didn't make it in time for supper, Mel,' he added between bites.

Food, however, was the last thing on Melissa's mind.

'You must have given it more thought than that,' she persisted. 'It wouldn't be like you to put it out of your head as if it was no concern of yours.'

'Which, strictly speaking, it wasn't,' Harris pointed out. 'It was up to Superintendent Thoroughgood how much importance was placed on the bits of information I was able to pass on.'

'I thought Holloway was in charge,' observed Iris from

her customary cross-legged position on the hearthrug. 'The way he chucks his weight about . . .'

Harris looked amused at the comment. 'He's done a lot of the spadework,' he agreed, 'but the Super's been leading the hunt for the Smiler.'

'But the Smiler turned out to be the "Daughters of Light",' said Melissa, 'and no one believed they'd killed Laura Maddox, did they?'

'No, but there had to be a connection somewhere, because of the smile. That was where I ran up against a brick wall as far as the Donovans were concerned. I didn't know about the drawings.'

'I knew that Natalie was given to obsessive doodling,' said Melissa. 'It was common knowledge in the art department, although Genty was quite definite she refused to show anyone her drawings.'

'Till Cluny dropped her in it by spilling them on the floor,' cackled Iris. 'Serve her right. Sorry for him, though,' she added, her voice unusually gentle.

'That was the first solid link between the Donovans and the Smiler,' Harris went on. 'And then Melissa reminded Genty about her claim that she'd never seen them. That threw her for a moment, although she recovered very quickly.'

'Her explanation was perfectly feasible,' Melissa pointed out. 'We know Natalie had been pressured not to blab about the smile, so she'd have been sure to beg Genty not to show her drawings to anyone else, or even admit to knowing about them.'

'Oh yes, it was feasible.' Harris agreed. He polished off the last of the sandwiches and beer, and wiped his mouth with a handkerchief. 'But when I pointed out that the date on the large drawing didn't tally with her account of when she received it, I could see she was rattled. And the sister was scared witless from the start, which made me certain I was on to something.'

'And so you decided to play the Laura Maddox card.'

'And Cluny put his foot in it again, in a big way,' remarked Iris sadly. 'Wonder if he realises what he's done. How's he taking it?' Her brow puckered in concern. 'Poor old boy. Really thought he was on smooth water again.'

'He's in shock, that's all I can say,' Harris replied. 'They got a doctor to him down at the station . . . he'll most likely spend the night in hospital, but in the long term, God knows what will become of him.'

'Perhaps his wife will come back. I wonder why she left home like that?' said Melissa.

'She might have known what the girls intended to do, but wanted no part of it,' said Harris. 'My guess is that they set about planning their revenge on Maddox soon after their brother's death. It wouldn't have been difficult to trace her . . . and when their doctor recommended a change of environment for Cluny, they were able to move close to where she lived without arousing suspicion. I'd love to know how they managed to get into the house without leaving any clues, how they knew when to strike and so on.'

'Maybe when the case comes to court . . .' began Iris.

'If it ever does,' he interrupted.

Both women looked at him in surprise and dismay. 'You think they might get away with it?' Iris exclaimed. 'But Genty confessed . . . we heard her.'

'That's not admissible evidence. If Genty refuses to repeat her confession at a formal interview, as any brief worth his salt would advise, and if Sirry and Cluny keep *stumm* as well, the police will have to come up with something far more concrete to pin the killings on them.'

'*Killings*?' Melissa exclaimed. 'Are you saying they've done it more than once?'

'Oh yes.' Harris's face was grim. 'Don't you remember Genty screaming, "Practice makes perfect"? I'll bet they copied that smile over and over again from Natalie's drawing. And then, because they'd been so programmed to practise everything, they even had to try out the actual murder on a substitute victim before going for the real thing. And there was someone ready to hand . . .'

'Oh, my God!' Melissa hardly recognised her own voice as the monstrous truth dawned on her. 'Martha Willis!'

'Unless I'm much mistaken. But unless they can be persuaded to admit it . . .' He broke off with a weary shrug, looking tired and despondent.

'I think perhaps it's time we went home,' said Melissa, and he got to his feet with evident relief.

'Next Saturday's your jumble sale, isn't it, Mel?' Iris said as she saw them out.

'Don't let Dorrie hear you call it that,' warned Melissa. 'Two o'clock at Carston Manor. Are you going?'

Iris fidgeted with the door handle and avoided eye contact as she replied 'If Jack agrees. He'll be here for the weekend.'

'That's nice,' said Melissa. 'What about you, Ken? It's a very high-class jumble sale,' she added, seeing him wince at the prospect, 'and it's worth going just to see the gardens.'

'I'll think about it,' he said. 'Goodnight Iris, thanks for the sarnies and beer.'

Back at Hawthorn Cottage, Melissa said, 'Iris is up to something.'

'What makes you say that?' asked Ken.

'I just have a feeling. She's been a bit cagey several times since her last trip to France. I wonder if it's anything to do with Jack.'

'Maybe he's persuaded her to make an honest man of him,' he suggested. 'Speaking of which . . .'

'No, Ken, we're not discussing that tonight.'

The 'Nearly New' sale in aid of Stowbridge Hospital was held in perfect April weather. Carston Manor and its grounds lay in a warm, sheltered valley where the spring was well advanced, splashing the grounds with bright flowers and masses of pink and white blossom against a background of tender green foliage. Supporters arrived in droves and swarmed through the downstairs rooms where Melissa, in company with Dorrie and the ladies of her committee, had worked for several days setting up racks and displaying the vast quantities of clothing that had been donated.

Florence and a team of helpers did a brisk trade in home-made cakes, preserves and refreshments, served from trestles set up in the old stone barn. Chairs were set out on the terrace for customers to rest and enjoy their tea while basking in the sunshine, admiring the gardens and watching the antics of the children on the bouncy castle, loaned for the occasion by a local firm and discreetly supervised by Tony.

Dorrie, every inch the lady of the manor, looked like a bright flower herself in a dress of daffodil yellow. Melissa and Ken, Iris and Jack, having dutifully made a number of purchases, sat on the terrace and watched her moving among the crowds, stopping here and there to chat, and smiling graciously at everyone.

'She does it to the manner born, as they say,' remarked Jack, who had heard Dorrie's story from Iris, under pain of unnamed penalties if he ever repeated it.

'I just hope no muck-raking journalist gets wind of her past,' said Melissa, after glancing round to make sure no one was within earshot, and the others nodded in agreement.

'Going to look round the garden,' Iris announced when she had finished her tea. 'Coming, Jack?'

Melissa watched them as they strolled among the flower beds. Iris held a handbag in one hand and with the other steadied her shady straw hat, which was threatened by a fitful breeze. Jack, hatless, his sturdy frame a head taller than hers, his square, honest face ruddy with health, walked beside her with his hands behind his back. There was no physical contact between him and Iris, yet their attitude, as from time to time they paused to inspect a plant or admire the water garden, indicated a peaceful pleasure in one another's company.

'He seems a nice chap,' said Ken, who was following her gaze. 'What does he do for a living.'

'He lectures at an agricultural college and he owns a small farm down in Somerset. He paints in his spare time – in fact, he was a student on one of Iris's courses in France a couple of summers ago. He fell for her on sight and they've been friends ever since . . . but she plays it very cool indeed,' Melissa added, smiling at the recollection of some typically 'Iris' remarks on the subject of Jack Hammond's devotion.

'Oh, yes?' Ken made the comment in a quizzical tone that made her turn to him in surprise.

'And what's that supposed to mean?'

'Just a thought.'

The reappearance of the two people under discussion prevented Melissa from pressing him any further. Jack said, 'I suggest we make a move. If we leave it much later it'll be chaos in the car park.'

The four of them had come together in Jack's car. When they reached Elder Cottage, he said to Melissa and Ken, 'We,' he glanced at Iris, who had turned slightly pink, 'would like you both to come for a drink with us presently. Say about six?'

'Why not?' said Melissa, after receiving a nod of agreement from Ken.

'See you later, then.'

Back in Hawthorn Cottage, Ken said, 'What did I tell you?'

'You don't know for certain.'

'You wait and see.'

'It's like this,' said Jack. 'I've taken early retirement. I've sold the farm and bought a property in Provence, and,' here he turned to Iris with a fond smile that made her go even pinker than before – 'Iris and I are going to settle there and establish an art school. After we're married, of course,' he added, taking his furiously blushing bride by the left hand, which she had hitherto been at pains to conceal, and displaying the sparkling solitaire.

'So that's why you've been so cagey recently!' exclaimed Melissa, after the couple had been congratulated and their health drunk.

'Had to wait till it was all settled,' said Iris, more relaxed now that the ordeal of the announcement was over.

'I suppose you'll be selling the cottage?' said Ken, glancing round the sitting-room with a look of appraisal.

'Thinking of making an offer?' asked Iris, with the wickedest of grins and a calculating gleam in her eye.

'You never know.' He turned to Melissa. 'I've booked a table at the *Manoir* for seven o'clock, so I think it's time we were leaving.'

On the way to the restaurant, he said, 'You're going to miss Iris, aren't you, Mel?'

After the euphoria of the engagement celebration, a sense of desolation swept over her. 'Oh Ken, you've no idea how I hate the thought of anyone else living in Elder Cottage,' she said sadly. 'I'm really happy for Iris – and Jack, of course – but I'm going to miss her dreadfully.'

There was a pause. Then he said, almost casually, his eyes fixed on the road, 'Those cottages could easily be knocked into one. They'd make a very comfortable home for two . . . with room for guests from the South of France or a son from New York.' He took one hand from the wheel and reached for hers. 'What do you say?'

She allowed her hand to rest in his. 'I'll think about it,' she replied softly.